# MARY CRAWFORD

# Rectify

## HIDDEN HEARTS BOOK 6

# COPYRIGHT

Published on April 22, 2017, by Diversity Ink Press and Mary Crawford. Publisher may be reached at MaryCrawfordAuthor.com.

ISBN: 978-1-945637-33-9


Cover by Covers Unbound

# HIDDEN BEAUTY SERIES

Until the Stars Fall from the Sky
So the Heart Can Dance
Joy and Tiers
Love Naturally
Love Seasoned
Love Claimed
If You Knew Me (and other silent musings) (novella)
Jude's Song
The Price of Freedom (novella)
Paths Not Taken
Dreams Change (novella)
Heart Wish (100% charity release)
Tempting Fate
The Letter
The Power of Will

# HIDDEN HEARTS SERIES

Identity of the Heart
Sheltered Hearts
Hearts of Jade
Port in the Storm (novella)
Love is More Than Skin Deep
Tough
Rectify
Pieces (a crossover novel)
Hearts Set Free
Freedom (a crossover novel)
The Long Road to Love (novella)
Love and Injustice (Protection Unit)
Out of Thin Air (Protection Unit)
Soul Scars (Protection Unit)

OTHER WORKS:
The Power of Dictation
Vision of the Heart
#AmWriting: A Collection of Letters to Benefit The
Wayne Foundation

# Dedication

Forgive yourself for what you can't change.
The past cannot be undone.
Hope lives in your ability
to do better
today.

# Chapter One

## Tayanita

THIRTEEN. IT DOESN'T SEEM possible that Ketki is thirteen. Yet, as she is trying to describe the game theory behind an arcade game to Shelby, the graces of womanhood are trying to overtake the child who was once there.

My child.

Ketki crosses her arms and scowls. "Mom! I told you to go right! Why did you go left?"

I suck in a breath as anguish slips past my carefully constructed mask.

Shelby shrugs. "I thought there was a shortcut there. So, sue me. I'm hungry anyway."

Mark rolls his eyes. "These days, it seems like I'm always feeding one or both of you. You guys are about to eat me out of house and home."

Shelby grins. "It's Ketki's birthday. We're supposed to be eating like there's no tomorrow. You ordered enough pizza to feed an army."

Mark bends down and kisses Shelby right in the middle of the pizza parlor as if there is not another soul

"

around. I have to look away as a soft bemused look crosses his face and he says, "You're right, there's nothing I like better than taking care of my girls. I love the fact that you watch out for Ketki."

I know Mark doesn't mean anything by those words, but they feel like a thousand scalpels to my heart.

I should be the one that Ketki calls Mom — but I'm not. I gave up that right.

I should be the one Mark is kissing — but I'm not. I gave up that right too.

I should be the one playing arcade games with Ketki — but I'm not. I forfeited that privilege more than a decade ago. Now, I sit on the sidelines and watch as another woman lives the life I gave up.

Most of the time, I can live with my choices. They were made a long time ago in a different place and time in a different state of mind. Then wasn't now. Today, it's all too hard to watch. Mark is a man who used to be my best friend and who is the kindest, most gentle man I ever knew — although he can be sharp-tongued and blunt at times. I watch with a profound sense of regret as he cuddles his new fiancé and gently kisses her as he watches our daughter's antics in the arcade. My heart squeezes painfully as I have to come to grips with the fact that the scene of domestic tranquility used to be my life. I had that life. I gave it up.

Over the years, I tucked that decision far away in the back of my mind. I tried to pretend the happily-ever-after white picket fence life that I once had and gave up never existed. I gave myself an imaginary lobotomy. I had the before and after version of Tayanita. That approach served me well for almost a decade; but then fate intervened. I have been thrown back into Mark's life and I can no longer pretend Mark and Ketki never existed.

Ketki exists in beautiful three-dimensional living color and it's been impossible to adequately explain to her what I don't quite understand myself. How do I explain to my inquisitive teenage daughter how I could walk away from her when she was not yet a toddler? How do I explain the debilitating effects of postpartum depression and the overwhelming impact of Mark's law school schedule on our lives? I completely lost myself and my identity in being a mother and I was sure I could never succeed. I had a dream of what being a mom was like and when it turned out not to be like that, I felt completely and utterly hopeless. There aren't enough words to explain the why.

Sure, I can put my nurse's hat on and explain it in some clinical fashion. I studied it extensively in school as I tried to solve the puzzle of me. I wanted to know why I wasn't like every other person I knew. I felt like a freak. Heck, I still feel like a freak as I watch Shelby, Mark and Ketki operate as the perfect nuclear family.

I'll be honest, when I first discovered who Shelby was, I wanted to hate her for being the person I couldn't be. Her experience as a teacher makes it easy for her to be a natural with Ketki. The two of them get along like two peas in a pod. You would never guess that they haven't known each other for a lifetime. Shelby doesn't even seem fazed by Ketki's odd style of interaction. She takes it in stride when Ketki won't make eye contact, flaps her hands, asks a million-and-a-half unrelated questions, or refuses to eat.

Most women would be completely freaked out by my presence in Mark's life. After all, I *am* the ex-wife and all that jazz, but Shelby has gone out of her way to include me and help me rebuild my relationship with both my ex-husband and my daughter. I mean … who does that? Over the years, I was waiting for the other shoe to drop to see if Shelby is really that nice — the answer is that she is. I know, I couldn't believe it myself for the longest time — but it seems to be true.

As I watch Shelby lean over and brush Ketki's hair out of her face in a completely natural gesture as she kisses her on the cheek, the pain is too much. I abruptly stand up and almost knock my stool over. The noise catches Ketki's attention and she asks, "Tayanita? What's wrong? Are you leaving? Why are you leaving? I thought you said you could stay for my whole birthday party? We haven't even had cake yet."

"Oh, I have to go. The hospital sent me a text message. They need me to come in," I fib in what I hope is a convincing manner.

Ketki narrows her gaze as she studies me carefully. "I don't think that's true. You told me earlier that you have a new person covering for you. You said you were going to be free all evening. Your eyelid is doing that weird twitchy thing it does when you don't want to tell me what's really happening. Whatever. If you don't want to be here, just go."

I walk over to where Ketki is as I try not to show how shaken I am by her accurate assessment of me. I carefully hug her as I say, "I'll catch you next time and we'll play your new video games, okay? Have a happy birthday. I love you, Ki."

Ever the gentleman, Mark stands up and shakes my hand as he brushes a kiss past my cheek. "Thank you for coming, Nita. It means a lot to us that you were here. I know it's difficult to get away from your job. So, thank you very much for trying."

There is no keeping polite distance from Shelby as she throws her arms around my neck and hugs me tight. "I can never thank you enough for your daughter. She is incredible. I love her so much and I love you for giving her life. In case no one has told you recently, you are amazing." As she pulls away and wipes her eyes, she adds, "Oh, don't forget I've got two students who are juniors. We are holding a little online career fair. Are you still available to talk about being a surgical nurse?"

I try to tamp down my wildly swinging emotions and come across as a logical, rational human being as I respond, "I don't know, let me figure out my schedule for the next couple weeks with the hospital and I'll see if I can be available."

Shelby nods. "Okay, sounds good. Send me a text message."

Ketki runs up to me briefly and hugs me around the waist as she says, "Tayanita, you know I'm a good listener. You can tell me what's really wrong."

I let out a gasp of air, although I'm not sure why I'm surprised. She says these types of things all the time. However, I'm usually not on the receiving end of them.

"I'll keep that in mind. For now, I need to run," I answer as I give my daughter a small squeeze and turn around and leave the room. The feeling of déjà vu is too much to bear.

My eyes are so swollen from crying I can barely see to insert the key as I open my front door. I throw my purse down on the kitchen table as I run to the bathroom. As I dim the lights and turn on the space heater, I run the hottest water I can stand in the big claw bathtub. The bathtub is why I bought this old historic house. It's about the only thing this old relic has going for it. Everything else has been a big money suck. I love that old tub with an almost obsessive passion.

It reminds me of my family. My grandma used to collect women's magazines dedicated to decorating and clip out all manner of pictures. She would save them for decades. Many of them featured these big porcelain tubs. When I began house hunting, I coveted these tubs as well. I never dreamed I'd own my own. My grandma would've been beside herself. I should have thought ahead before purchasing this gigantic house, but once my heart was sold on this tub, very little about the rest of the house mattered to me.

As I'm about to climb in my cherished tub, my phone rings with a tone so shrill it could peel paint off the wall. I keep my cell phone ring tone annoying for a very precise reason. As a surgical nurse I'm often on-call in the event of an emergency. I recently received a promotion to be the head of my unit which means if someone calls in sick, I am on call to make sure there is always someone available. I simply don't have the luxury to ignore phone calls. I shut off the water, wrap a towel around myself and run to answer the phone in the kitchen.

My voice is so hoarse from crying I barely recognize my voice. "Hello?" I dance a little on the cold tile floor as I start to shiver.

"Good evening, ma'am, this is John. I'm calling from Right Side Up Vinyl Siding Company, and I've called to let you know you have been randomly selected to receive two hundred dollars' worth of free siding."

"John, I hate to tell you this ... but there isn't anything I'm less interested in than vinyl siding."

There are about five seconds of dead silence and then a very loud guffaw of laughter before he asks, "Nothing? Not even having to judge whether toenail fungus cream is effective?" he asks.

"Believe it or not, I routinely face more disgusting things in my job."

"Let me tell you, this job is no picnic either. Some days I have to sell male enhancement products. You're lucky I didn't happen to call yesterday."

"Okay, I'll concede the point. That doesn't sound fun. Let's face it though, it could be worse, you could be the guy who cleans out porta-potties."

"Maybe cold calling isn't the worst job on the planet, but getting vinyl siding isn't the worst thing that can happen to you either. I mean, you could be a human test dummy for pepper spray and have to take a warm shower afterward."

"Ooh, you have a sadistic streak," I laugh. "Okay, how about this: would you rather be a deodorant tester and have to tell beautiful women and men who look like Adonis they have body odor? Wouldn't that be more difficult than selling plastic stuff that goes on people's houses?"

There is another long pause on the other end of the phone. "If siding was the only thing I sold, it might not be so bad. But, I basically have to sell whatever comes across my desk. One day it might be siding and another day it might be tickets to a charity concert for teen mothers with anorexia. Still other times it's embarrassing products like male enhancement products, hair regrowth or some random diet thing —"

"So, you're required to be an expert on these things? Do you even get a chance to try out the products before you have to pitch them to total strangers?"

John chokes back a gust of laughter. "I'm not sure how you meant that. I don't try most of the products I have to pitch. Some of this stuff is downright creepy. I don't make enough money to try the majority of the stuff I sell."

I groan aloud. "Oh my Gosh, I didn't even mean it the way it sounded. I'm completely stressed out. I've had the world's worst day ever."

I can hear John take a sip of something before he says, "Look, I'm supposed to be selling you a boatload of vinyl siding right now and I don't feel like having twenty or thirty other people hang up on me at the moment, so we'll pretend this is a normal sales call and I will listen to you tell me why your day was so terrible, okay? Does that sound like a plan?"

"John, you don't know me and I don't know you. I don't think you want to know all the things wrong in my life right now. I would probably bore you to tears. I can almost guarantee by the time we're done you'll think I am a disgusting human being. Are you sure you're up to all that?"

"It sure beats having what seems like half of humanity cuss me out and call me the lowest form of pond scum for interrupting their French fries, Big Macs, and pizza."

"Okay, I hear where you're coming from. That would really suck. So, in an effort to save you from further suckage in your life, I'll tell you about what's going on in mine. Since you don't know me from Adam, you are free to be as judge-y as you want to be — because you know what, I don't give a flying fig's butt about what you think of me because I'm never going to talk to you again."

"Sounds like a plan … Wait. What should I call you? You never told me your name."

"Since you're playing 'Dear Abby' tonight … I can't tell you my name. I don't have a name — for tonight's purposes I'm anonymous." I look down at the blue towel I'm wearing and whisper into the phone like one of those over-the-top TV actresses and comment, "You can call me the 'Lady in Blue'"

John laughs out loud as he says, "Okay, if that's how you want to play it, I'm good with that. So what brings you to John's Advice Line tonight? Although I have to tell you I'm not exactly qualified to give advice and my suggestions may or may not be any good — but as long as you're okay with that, I'm your man."

"It's funny that you mentioned pizza before. It's what caused my existential crisis tonight."

"Yeah, I always feel the same way when I am facing down the second half of a pizza."

"Sadly, this is much, much more serious than simply controlling my appetite. Actually, you're right. The pizza wasn't the issue at all. It was the background scenery. I'm the issue; I've always been."

"I'm sure it wasn't that bad. How bad could things be if there was pizza involved, right?"

"No, there's no sugarcoating this, it's bad."

"Oh, come on, it can't be much worse than what I do. I call perfect strangers and try to sell them stuff they probably can't afford and don't need. It's not like I'm the pillar of society or anything — I'm not curing kids of cancer or rescuing kittens from a burning house or anything heroic."

"I don't know John, trying to sell me vinyl siding probably doesn't equate to all the bad things I've done in my life. I've done things I doubt I'll forgive myself for."

"Well, I'm sorry to tell you this, my Lady in Blue, if you haven't done something in your life you're ashamed of, you probably haven't lived a very full life. I think we're all in a position where we would've done something different if we would've known better."

There is a small portion of my heart that warms at his reassurance, but then my common sense hits and I can't set aside my guilt. "I wish I could rationalize away what I've done with a few well-reasoned platitudes, but I can't."

"That sounds intense. No wonder you were crying into your pizza! Why don't you tell me what's going on? It might make you feel better."

"This is crazy, I don't even know why I am telling you this —" I am interrupted by a shrill sound on the other end of the phone.

"Crap! Joey Smits was probably smoking in the bathroom again. I gotta go. I hate this. I could've talked to you all night."

"So, this is it? I won't get to speak to you again?"

"No, I'm not saying that. I don't know. I'll try to figure it out, but the managers are here evacuating our offices. This place is like a dry tinderbox. I gotta jet. You made my whole day. I'm sorry to have to leave it like this, Lady in Blue."

I draw in a quick breath. "Take care of yourself John, you made my day too. I'm getting in the bathtub now before my water gets much colder. I know most people get angry when you call, but you made me feel much better. Thank you."

"Well, Lady in Blue you gave me a visual to help sustain me for a long while. Thank you for that."

# CHAPTER TWO

# JOHN

I AM NOT A happy camper. The single best conversation I've had in months was blown to pieces because two of our new hires decided it would be fun to get frisky in the bathroom and smoke some weed. Now, I'm not an old fuddy-duddy. But, if you're going to be stupid, don't set off the smoke alarm. It messes with everybody's day.

Derek, the guy responsible for babysitting me this week, walks me back to my desk and guides my hands to my armrest on the chair.

As I sit back down in my chair and hit the button on my phone for the readout on the telephone number, I find the queue is empty. Derek must still be standing by and able to read my facial expressions because he asks, "What's wrong, man?"

"There's something wrong with my phone, it's not recalling the last few numbers I dialed." I rake my hand through my hair in frustration.

"Didn't you fill out a contact sheet?" Derek asks and then thinks better of it. "Oh never mind, I forgot you don't do it that way."

"Yeah, I'm still new to brailing and it's not effective

for as many calls as we take."

"Look, it's no big deal. You'll get another one. You're good at this. Make some more calls — it's what we do."

"Derek, all I'm asking is can you retrieve the freakin' number for me? Is that too much to ask? Can you star ninety-nine or whatever it is you do?"

"Okay, relax. I'm not one of your soldiers under your command. A little please might go a long way. I've got a couple codes that might work. Otherwise, you'll have to wait until our performance reports come out in a few days to see who you called. You spent a while on the line with this person, right? The number should pop up on the top of the list."

I breathe a sigh of relief. At least I have a backup plan. I hate those stupid performance matrixes with a passion. We're tracked of every minute of every day as if we're mice running in a maze. Yet, that stupid report may end up being my salvation.

I can hear Derek pushing buttons on my phone and then heave a huge sigh. "No dice, man. When they cut the power to turn off the smoke alarm system, it must have wiped out the memory in the phone system. I'm sorry you lost your big fish, hope it doesn't hurt your numbers too much. I was hoping you could beat Billy Taylor. He's been the employee of the month far too many times for my taste. He needs to be knocked down a notch or two."

I grimace at Derek's comment knowing Billy sits a couple desks away from me and can probably hear every word Derek is saying. I don't need any unnecessary drama between my coworkers. I can't say Derek is wrong either. I just don't need him to be starting a pissing war at my desk.

I nod in Derek's direction. "Thanks for trying to help. I appreciate it. There's nothing like taking an unscheduled break in the middle of the parking lot to ruin your momentum."

"No problem, Dude. Let me know if you need anything."

I clip my earpiece in and adjust the microphone. "Well, it was worth a shot, I'm sorry I lost that number. I guess I better get to calling people or I'll never get a shot at employee of the month."

Derek claps me on the shoulder. "Things could be worse. We could be selling air conditioning units in the middle of December."

I smile. "You know … you are not the first person to remind me that this isn't the worst job in the universe."

As I adjust the seat belt in the taxi, my phone rings. Fumbling with my phone, I pick it up, "Go for John," I habitually answer.

"Jonathan Thomas Ashford, I don't know why you can't tell your mother 'hello' like a normal person. It's strange how you answer the phone."

"I'm sorry, Mom. All those years in the military are hard to undo."

"How did your last visit to the doctor go? Do you think there's any hope they'll let you back in the service?"

"Mom, I know you mean well, but the Coast Guard doesn't have any use for a blind guy."

"You know, your dad thinks you should sue. He

read a newspaper article the other day about somebody who got millions of dollars from their employer because they slipped on a wet floor."

"It'd be nice, but I can't do that. When I 'upped' with the guard, I knew there would be risks. I was too close to that helicopter blade. Nobody expected there to be a glitch in the wiring. It was a freak accident. It simply started spinning when it shouldn't have."

"Still, it's unfair. You're my baby and you are tough. A bump on the head shouldn't have caused you to go blind," my mom protests.

"I know. That's what makes this a freak accident all around. According to my ophthalmologist, I had several risk factors too. If I hadn't already been a smoker with high blood pressure on the high side, I might've escaped the concussion with no problems. Aneurysms are random. They can strike at any time. Some people can be severely impacted, while other people have no lasting effects."

"So that's it? They're just giving up?" my mom pushes one more time.

I sigh. "Mom, I don't know what to tell you. I got hit in my occipital lobe and it burst an aneurysm behind my eyes. It ruptured when the helicopter blade hit me. It's unusual for someone my age to have it, but I guess my blood vessels may have been weakened by the years I spent smoking. I've got no vision in my left eye and next to no vision in my right. They don't know if I'll ever get it back, but as time passes, the chances of me getting my vision restored are progressively less. I take blood pressure medicine to lower my risk of having another aneurysm. It could have been much, much worse, I guess."

"I'm sorry, Johnny. I worry about you. I don't think you're eating right and you never go out with your friends anymore. You seem to hate your job, and you don't even go to church with your father and me."

"I know, Mom. I don't mean to worry you. I'm just having a little trouble figuring out who I am since the accident. I used to be so sure of myself, I even bordered on cocky, and now everything is just harder."

"I'm sorry it's so difficult, but will you at least come over and celebrate your sister's birthday? It would mean a lot to her."

"Yeah, I wouldn't miss Kate's birthday for anything," I say. "I'll be there for sure. She still likes chocolate, right?"

"She does, but I'm not sure about her boyfriend. She's bringing her new beau. I guess this one's name is Vincent. She says he's the real deal. She warned us to be nice to him."

I chuckle softly. "When am I ever not nice to her boyfriends?"

"Well, you did flash your military ID at that one guy —"

"You have to agree, the guy was a complete jerk. If he took it to mean I was the military police, that's his fault and not my problem."

"Come to think of it, Katie was glad you scared that one off," my mom concedes. "What about you? Are you bringing anyone to the birthday party?" My mom sounds hopeful.

All I can say is it's a good thing the taxi driver has

his headphones on and isn't paying attention to this conversation because I can't believe my mom is grilling me about my dating life at my age. I feel like I'm about fifteen. I roll my eyes so hard she can probably see the gesture through the telephone. "No Mom, I'm not dating anybody right now — but I met somebody nice through work."

I can hear my mom shift on the other end of the phone and bring it closer to her mouth as she asks me, "What's her name?"

It's a good thing my mom cannot see me blush bright red as I have to admit, "Well, there's a funny story behind that … but I don't know."

"Jonathan Ashford! What kind of place are you working at?"

I swallow a snort of surprise laughter as I answer, "Mother! Get your mind out of the gutter!"

"Well, with an introduction like that, an imagination can go wild."

"Trust me. It's not as juicy as you're thinking. You probably need to cut back on those reality television shows you're watching."

"Okay, sorry. Go on with your story."

"Well, there's not much of a story. I called her as part of my job — today it was selling vinyl siding. She has the most intriguing voice. It's lyrical and sexy with great humor. She's not afraid to laugh at herself and the joke. She's sassy and funny. I can tell she is incredibly smart."

"You could tell all this from a discussion about vinyl siding?" my mom asks skeptically.

"Obviously we didn't spend the whole time talking

about siding."

"You didn't talk about her name either, so what did you talk about?"

"Lots of random stuff about life. Unfortunately, we got interrupted by the fire alarm, so I never got around to asking her. She had me call her the Lady in Blue."

"Oh, how intriguing! I bet she reads a lot and likes mysteries. So, when are you going to see this lovely lady again?"

"Well, Mom, that's where fate is not my friend. I don't even know if I'll be able to find her again. All I know about her that is I love the sound of her voice, her laugh and her wonderful sense of humor. I couldn't get her phone number after a mishap at work. We tried to retrieve it, but they turned off the power to turn off the smoke alarm and it vanished from the phone's memory."

"So, that's it? You can't remember the number you called or anything like that?" my mom laments, "This is like something from one of my soap operas. Real life can't be like that."

"Yeah … well … recently my luck has not been the best. Maybe this was not meant to be."

"You know, I can't bring myself to believe that, even after all the bad things that happened to you. So, I'll make sure to set a plate for you on Sunday, okay?"

Walking with a white cane is so demoralizing. It's like advertising to the world that I can't see. However, it has become a necessity if I want to leave my house. I am a far cry from the elite athlete I once was. I can barely make it up the porch steps of my parents' house without tripping and falling. Hearing my sister shriek my name makes it worth all the effort it took me to get dressed and wrap her present this morning though.

"I can't believe you made it all the way here!" my sister says as she grabs my neck and gives me a hug.

"Yeah, Greyhound is a miraculous jump forward in technology," I deadpan.

"Shut up! You know what I mean. You were always too busy before." My sister punches me lightly on the arm. "Did you bring me a present?"

"Of course I did, I've been your big brother for many years now. I know I wouldn't dare come to your birthday party without a present. You would skin me alive."

Another voice enters the conversation, "I see I'm not the only guy you have wrapped around your little finger, Katie-dyd."

*Crap, they're already at the cute nickname stage. I wonder how long she's been dating this one?*

My sister reaches out and places my hand in someone else's as she says, "Johnny, I would like you to meet my boyfriend Vinnie, I call him Vinnie the Pooh."

As he clears his throat and shakes my hand he corrects, "It's nice to meet you, sir. My name is actually Vincent Hurlington."

"It's nice to meet you Vincent. You don't have to call me sir. I'm not in the military anymore — John is fine."

"So, your vision impairment is expected to be long-term then?" he asks with a tone of open curiosity.

"Vinnie, don't be rude. He doesn't like to talk about that stuff."

"No, I'm not trying to be rude. I noticed you walk with a cane. I'm wondering if you've ever thought about having a service dog. My sister works at a place. They used to be headquartered in Kansas, but they recently moved back to Florida. They got new offices in Gainesville. They train all sorts of dogs. Have you ever thought about getting one?"

"Sure, I've thought about it tons of times, but I always thought the waiting list for those kinds of dogs was years and years long. I figured since we weren't sure my vision would ever get better it wouldn't be fair for me to put myself on one of those lists. I suppose I should probably think about it sometime soon. The doctors don't think I am likely to see any improvement anytime soon. I guess I need to be shifting my mindset around a little."

"Well, I'll give you Zoe's phone number and you can talk to her, but I've seen some of the stuff their dogs do and it's impressive."

My sister squeezes my hand. "Oh John, wouldn't that be the best? It would mean you could get out and go hiking again. That would be the perfect birthday present for me. I hope you can get together with his sister and work something out."

"It will be something worth looking into for sure. Do you mind pointing me toward the kitchen? I've been looking forward to mom's meatloaf for days. I'm sorry to break it to you Squirt, you think I came to see you — but actually I'm here for the food."

My sister laughs. "What makes you think I'm not? I

grew up in the same household you did. Who do you think asked Mom to make it? I'm the birthday girl, I get to set the menu, remember?"

"That was a stroke of genius if you ask me. Good thinking, Katie. Did you ask for corn and mashed potatoes on the side?"

"Of course, I would never go halfway. So, tell me about the new job," she asks as we walk toward the kitchen. I almost don't need her help — but my parents have done enough changing in here that I don't trust my judgment quite enough to do it by memory.

As I sit down on the vinyl chair, I confess to Katie, mostly, it's like being stabbed in the ego a thousand times a day. "People don't like to talk to telephone solicitors. Mostly I get cussed out. But occasionally, there's a funny story."

"Yeah? Care to share?" Katie asks.

"Well, you know I sell something different almost every day. So it can be anything from concert tickets for a charity cause to male enhancement products to vinyl siding."

"You've mentioned that before. That must be awkward."

"Most of the time it is, but sometimes it can be kind of funny. The other day I was selling some generic hearing aid substitutes. This little old man who couldn't hear me even though I was shouting on the phone handed his phone to his neighbor. It turns out they live in a duplex and she went ahead and bought them for him because she was tired of hearing him watch X-rated movies on his television set at the top volume. It was one of the most successful days I've had in a while. I felt bad for him though. He was so embarrassed she could hear what he was watching — I guess he didn't realize it was quite so loud."

"I'm so proud of you, my big brother always in service to your country whether officially … or not," my sister says with a smirk in her voice.

Although Kate said it in jest, I can't help but wonder how my Lady in Blue is doing since I didn't get a chance to follow up with her.

I must be wearing my worry all over my face because my mother looks over at me and says, "Johnny, what's wrong? I thought meatloaf was one of your favorites."

I smile up at her as she arranges the food on my plate. "No worries, Mom. I'm just thinking about work and life. It's great to be home for a change."

# Chapter Three

# Tayanita

I TAKE A MOMENT to blow on my coffee during my break and relax. I hear a staticky, disembodied voice over the intercom system say, "T. Moya, please report to room 104J as soon as possible."

*Crap!* I was two minutes late this morning. It wasn't even my fault. Somebody's dog crawled through a car window on the interstate and went for a run. Cars everywhere had stopped to try to catch this dog before it became a casualty. Fortunately, I had a couple bologna sandwiches in my lunch, so I lured him to my car. I stopped off at Jessica and Mitch's place and drop the pup off because he didn't have any tags, and I had no way of knowing which car he came from. Mitch and Stuart will make sure he gets reunited with his owner. That's one of the things they do at Hope's Haven. Even so, the side trip made me late. I can't believe they're essentially calling me to the principal's office for being two minutes late. I am never, *ever* tardy — I'm always early. This is crazy.

I reluctantly step into the Chief Medical Officer's office and try not to show that my knees are shaking inside my scrubs. The only other two times I've been in here was when another nurse was stealing medication and wrongly pointed the finger at me. Fortunately, the operation was being filmed and all the evidence cleared me. The other time I was here was recently when I earned a promotion to shift supervisor. As that thought crosses my mind, my stomach drops to my feet. Maybe I'm not performing well enough and they want to take that promotion back. I hope that's not the case — because I enjoy being the supervisor and showing the newer nurses the ropes.

I sit on my hands to avoid chewing on my fingernails. Over the years, I've tried a million things to break myself of that habit. As a kid, I used to go into the garden and rub the juice of hot peppers on my fingers because my grandma used to tell me that was the most effective thing to do. It used to burn so bad it made me cry. Unfortunately, it didn't make me stop chewing my nails.

I look down and notice my knee is bouncing as if I am guilty already. I need to stop acting as if I've been condemned. I don't even know why I am here.

Finally, Dr. Knightley comes in and sits on the corner of his desk. The fact he's so purposefully trying to be friendly unnerves me. Usually, he's much more formal.

"Good morning, Nurse Moya. How are you this morning?"

"A little nervous that I'm going to get fired," I blurt before I can stop myself.

Dr. Knightley's eyebrows rise toward the ceiling. "Why? Do I have reason to?"

"No, absolutely not. It's just that you're not known for asking nurses to your office for coffee."

Dr. Knightley's eyebrows furrow as he ponders my statement. "Hmm, perhaps you're right. Maybe I should do that more often. People do seem to be a little afraid to come visit me. Nevertheless, I did not invite you here to fire you. By all accounts, you seem to be doing an exemplary job. You have an excellent eye for detail and you are a natural-born teacher."

I flush a little as I hear his words. I was not expecting a compliment. In fact, that was the last thing I was anticipating today. "Thank you, sir. I try very hard."

Dr. Knightley clears his throat and picks up a file from his desk. "That's what makes this all the much more difficult to say."

"Oh no, is it a reduction-in-force? Am I being laid off? I just got that promotion —" I speculate, unable to keep my thoughts from erupting.

"No, I'm afraid it's a little more serious than that. We are still trying to sort it all out, but it appears a patient flat-out lied to us. Either we missed it on the blood screening, or records were mixed up. We were later contacted by the family of the patient who had the emergency femoral laceration repair you assisted on the other day —"

"Oh, you mean the one that squirted me in the face through my mask? That was lovely. I barely had time to get my face mask up," I comment sarcastically.

Dr. Knightley looks down at the paperwork as he says, "The surgical record says you were hit directly in the eye, is that correct?"

"Yeah, I went to the eyewash station and followed all the protocols," I answer with a sigh. "He caught me off guard, he bled like a geyser. I haven't made that kind of mistake since I was a rookie. I put all my notes in the file. Why do you need to know? Are they threatening to sue me? I thought that patient pulled through okay."

"No, I think it's the other way around. I think his family is afraid you might sue them because he didn't disclose the fact he was HIV-positive."

"No, that's not possible. I examined his chart myself. There wasn't anything about that on the chart. It should have been there. I crossed-typed the blood. I looked close enough to make sure there weren't any allergies. There was nothing," I insist, as the horror of it all sinks in.

"I know, Ms. Moya. That's the part of this we're trying to figure out. In the meantime, consider whether you want to start a course of antivirals. Even though you followed proper protocol for blood exposure, it may not be quite enough given the added risk factor that we are now aware of," Dr. Knightley says as he offers me a tissue and a little Dixie cup of water.

"What do I do now?" I stare up at him blankly.

"I've arranged for someone else to come in and work your shift today — don't worry, you'll still be paid. I think you probably need a little time to process the news. Scientifically, the chances of transmission of this HIV virus — given the precautions you took are slim. I know that's small comfort but it's true."

My head swims and I tremble as I glance over at Dr. Knightley. "I'm sorry I need to go. Maybe someday I'll be able to talk about this rationally, but today is not that day."

Dr. Knightley stands up and pats me on the shoulder as he walks me out the door. "Understood, Nurse Moya. Do you have family I can call for you? It seems to me that it would be a good idea for you to be around someone right now."

"You're probably right, but I don't have anybody to

call. Thanks for asking though."

Sitting in the middle of my floor with only Mr. Whiskers to keep me company, I decide to call Shelby. She's the only person in my life who comes close to understanding what I'm facing.

I wait as it seems like it takes forever for her to pick up the phone. When she finally answers, I ask, "Is Ketki there?"

Shelby seems a little confused by the odd tone of my voice as she answers, "No, I'm sorry you missed her. Mark took her to go get some ice cream."

"That's great. I want to talk to you anyway," I admit in a rush.

"Oh, just a minute. Let me get the file about career day."

"No, I didn't call to talk business," I answer after a long pause. "I called because I want you to get drunk with me."

"Tayanita, I think I need an explanation."

"Why? I'm free, you're white and we're both over twenty-one." I snort with an uncharacteristically loud laugh.

"Mmm-hmm, I see. You're already a couple ahead of me, aren't you?"

"Oh, prolly. I was talking to Mr. Whiskers and decided I was too young to die. If anybody knows about that, I figured it was prolly you."

"Oh boy, it sounds like there's a story there. I'll tell you what, I'm going to go grab Savannah and maybe some aspirin then we'll be right over. In the meantime, how about you try to mix it up with some water until we get there?"

"Does Savvy have to come? I mean she's nice and all, but every time I'm around her I'm reminded she's together with the most perfect guy, and I always feel stupid. Around the two of you, I feel like the pathetic third wheel who can't even get a date."

"I agree, Casey is pretty great. There was more than one time in Savannah's life where she thought she would die, so she's been in our shoes. Besides, we need someone there because someone needs to be the designated driver."

"Okay, but the two of you are not allowed to brag all night about how perfect your life is. Got it?"

"Pinky swear," Shelby vows. "We'll be right there."

As I sit in my big round wicker chair and hug a throw pillow, Savannah brings over a tray of food and sets it in front of me. "The guy I'm not supposed to mention made this and he said to tell you the green salsa is a lot hotter than the red, so proceed with caution."

I stare at her blankly and blink as it takes a while for her words to penetrate my rattled brain. "Oh, you mean Casey. I didn't mean you couldn't say his name like he was Voldemort or something. I don't want you guys to talk about sweet syrupy things or how hot your guys are in bed. I can't even remember the last time I had someone else besides my cat in my bed. It's getting depressing. I guess I won't have to worry about it too much longer."

Shelby pulls the ottoman closer to where I am and

sits on it as she says, "This is the second time you've said something like that to me. What gives?"

I heave a dry sarcastic laugh. "You know what's funny? When I was a little girl, I used to look at my grandma with all her wrinkles and say to myself, 'I never want to get that old'. I don't want those lines on my face or those age spots and I don't want my hair to turn silver. It was so against my culture to think that way too. We're taught to respect our elders and hold them in high esteem, but when I was younger, all I could think was how wrinkled and fragile my grandma looked and how I didn't want to be like her. Now, it seems like my wish might actually come true. I might not even get close to old age. I'm not even thirty yet. I'm too young to die."

"Nita, did you go to the doctor or something? What's going on? Why are you talking like this? This is not like you."

I can't help myself as I let out another burst of angry laughter. "I guess you could say I saw a doctor today. Now, let me tell you it wasn't my idea. I was summoned to the CMO's office this morning between surgeries — well, that's not exactly right either. Following my first surgery, I was sent home after he basically told me there's a chance I may have been handed a death sentence by simply doing my job."

"That's awful. What do you mean exactly?" Savannah asks softly.

"I feel so stupid. You don't go to nursing school without knowing what the risks are. So, I should've known this was a possibility, but if you know me you know I'm one of the most careful, methodical nurses out there. I don't go into surgery without reading the chart front to back, top to bottom, inside out. My hands are quick and I practice with every new instrument until I can use them in my sleep and work with them blind."

"I know you're a good nurse, I've been under your care, remember? I've heard what the doctors have to say about you. All I can say is it's very clear where Ketki gets some of her mannerisms from. You two are a lot alike — and that's a good thing."

I scrub my hands down my face. "Oh my Gosh, this will be so hard on her. I just came into my daughter's life; it would be the ultimate twist of cruelty if I were to die."

"I still don't understand. If you're so careful, why do you think you're going to die?" Savannah asks.

"I'm prolly not supposed to tell you guys any of this stuff. But suffice it to say there are lotsa ways to be exposed to blood-borne pathogens in a hospital and I got hit with one of the most obscure ones."

"Blood-borne pathogens?" Shelby asks with alarm. "Are you talking about the Ebola virus?"

"No, I guess I can thank my lucky stars that isn't the problem, or at least I don't think that's the problem. This virus is much older — it was big in the 80s"

"You were exposed to AIDS?" Savannah asks incredulously. "I thought everybody who was infected with HIV was on fancy medications like Magic Johnson. Hasn't he lived with his for a couple of decades now?"

"You're a freaking genius. I was so upset I didn't even think to ask about his treatment protocol. That would reduce my risk for sure. All I can do now is wait for the results of my blood test to come back."

"So, we've got the food my brother-in-law made, some delicious iced tea, and Savvy and I are here all night until someone comes to get us. What's on the agenda for the girls' night?"

I scoop up a chip with salsa and sour cream and pop it in my mouth. After I stall as long as possible by making a huge production of chewing it, swallowing and taking a large drink of iced tea, I look at both of them and shrug as I admit, "Look, I know I said I didn't want to talk about men tonight, but I have to tell you about this guy, John."

Both women lean forward in their seats as they say simultaneously, "We have to hear about this."

I practically scream in frustration as I throw my hands in the air. "The story is, I have nothing to say about John because the only thing I know about him is that he has a super sexy voice, a wicked sense of humor, and apparently a heart the size of Texas because he was going to listen to my whole sob story the other night without even knowing who I was, because he could tell I was completely freaking out."

Savannah gets a murderous look on her face as she asks, "Tell me the guy didn't tell you he would listen to you and then turn around and bail on you?"

"Well, that's exactly what he did — but it wasn't his fault. The smoke alarms went off in his office when he was talking on the phone with me he had no choice but to evacuate."

"That's too bad. He called you back the next day, didn't he?" Shelby asks.

"No, he hasn't. That leaves you to wonder if maybe I hallucinated the whole incident because I was under so much stress," I muse. "These days, I don't know who I am, where I've been or what direction I'm headed. I don't even trust my senses to tell me what's real and what's imagined anymore."

# CHAPTER FOUR

# JOHN

I DON'T KNOW IF McFerran has an extra door open or if he keeps an air conditioner on in his office, but my boss's office is about twenty degrees colder than the rest of the building. I fight to keep my expression neutral as I wait for him to do whatever it is he's doing rather than talking to me. What little vision I have left only allows me to see large shapes under extremely bright conditions. In this dim environment, I'm as good as completely blind. I doubt I'll ever get used to the feeling of complete isolation in a public place.

I clear my throat in frustration. With my luck, Mike McFerran will interpret it as a sign of nervousness.

I hear the squeak of his chair as he turns in my direction and says, "Ashford, I forgot you were there. You gotta learn to speak up. Did you go mute when you went blind?"

I have to remind myself I'm not in the Coast Guard anymore and I cannot simply order this UNT hipster to mind his manners and be respectful. He has no idea what it's like to live in my shoes.

"It could be because I was waiting for you to tell me

what this meeting is about. I figured you might know since you're the one who called it. I can't very well talk about what I don't know." I bite the inside of my cheek to keep from saying more.

"Hofstetter told me you wanted a copy of your production numbers. That makes me curious. The whole time you've been here you've never wanted to know how well you did. I figured you didn't give a crap. Why now?"

"Honestly? Our little unscheduled fire drill the other day interrupted a call with a potential client. She's the homeowner, and she seemed interested in siding. I was planning to wrap up the sale," I reply in an attempt to sound utterly disinterested in the contents of the report on his desk.

"You puzzle me, Ashford. You act like you don't give a rat's butt about this job. Yet, you show up here every day and get it done. You're not my top guy, but you still pull in great numbers. But I can't help but think you completely detest this job."

"With all due respect, I do."

I can hear McFerran draw in a sharp breath. "Listen, you ungrateful son of a puke, I didn't have to hire you in the first place. I only did it because I get tax breaks for having you here. You're lucky you even have a job."

His words confirm every fear I've had since becoming disabled. In fact, they pretty much spell out my every nightmare. I used to be a heroic person who rescued people. Since when did I become the object of pity and disdain? I carefully take a drink from my bottle of soda before I formulate an answer. The benign activity gives me a socially acceptable reason to take a few moments to calm down before I speak.

I take a deep breath and prepare to talk, but it's surprisingly disconcerting to not be able to read another person's body language. "It completely blows, but you're right … I am lucky to have a job. A lot of visually impaired folks don't. Unfortunately, you forgot to mention the other part of the equation. You are darned lucky to have *me*. I don't know if you bothered to read the resume the Veteran's Administration sent over, but I have a bachelor's degree in Geology, which I earned with honors, and I did so well in flight school with the Coast Guard I have clearance to shuttle the President of the United States of America around if needed."

"Well, la-de-da. All that and a five-dollar bill might get you a burger at a fast food joint somewhere. It doesn't do you any good now."

"How kind of you to bring that to my attention. Do you think I don't notice it every single freakin' day? But as someone I know pointed out to me recently, this isn't the worst job on the planet. So, if you'll give me my performance report, I'll get back to it."

I hear paper rustling before he shoves something in my hands. "I don't know what you're gonna do with this anyway. You can't read the danged thing."

"Don't worry about it. It's not your problem. I've got it taken care of."

McFerran kept me in his office so long I almost missed Derek. I rush past the banks of phones in our cramped cubicle-like spaces. My progress comes to an abrupt stop when I catch the tip of my cane on Beverly Ann's lunch bag and almost topple over and land in her lap. *Crap! I*

*hate when stuff like this happens.*

I hear her mutter, "Hey idiot, watch where you're going!"

As I am about to apologize for the mishap, Derek runs up and slides his hand under my elbow as he remarks, "Whoa! Dude, you should've waited for me to come back and help you. My girlfriend has to work late tonight anyway. I've got loads of time." He tends to let his mouth run a little, but at heart — he is a nice kid. Kid? Who am I kidding? He's probably not much younger than me. I feel several centuries old these days. I'm not even thirty-three, but I feel ancient.

"So… What are your plans for this very long weekend?" Derek asks.

"I hadn't planned anything special. I got a new audiobook I might try out," I say. "Hey, before you leave, can you look at this and see if you can figure out the number of the call that got interrupted last week?"

Derek pokes me in the shoulder taking me by surprise as he says, "I see how this goes. You're going to be a smooth operator and try to get yourself a date for some Netflix and chill this weekend."

I shake my head as I scoff, "No, I don't think that's how this will go. I'm going to call her and talk about some siding."

"Dude, do I look like a moron? If you are that interested in tracking down a number, there's more involved than just siding. Customers come and go in our business. We get handed hundreds and hundreds of numbers every day. There's something special about this one. You're swimming in some river called 'de Nile'. But, I'll play along."

"Great. Lunch is on me whenever you want."

"Dude, you've forgotten how much I can eat. Don't worry about it, hand me your phone."

I give him my phone and I hear him punching in numbers. Finally, he asks me, "What should I call this contact?"

I shrug nonchalantly. "I guess I'll color-code it and call it Blue."

Derek shifts his position and punches a few more buttons on the phone. "Whatever. I won't question your organizational system." He hands my phone back as he adds, "Hey, don't forget we're off this whole week for Thanksgiving. We don't have to come back until Monday. McFerran decided he didn't want to face the wrath of customers being disturbed while they sat down for their turkey dinner. Go have some fun or something. Eat some awesome food. You know … take a vacation. Stop thinking so hard about life."

I chuckle softly. "I was in the military so long I don't remember what a vacation is."

"Now is as good a time as any to remember," Derek suggests.

"Sounds like a plan," I respond with a smile.

"You can say that again. You have no idea the righteous plans I have in store for my girl. I'm going to make her so happy she'll fart rainbows."

I grin. "Well, I hope your mission goes as planned and both of our vacations are not a huge SNAFU."

As the sun warms my face, I sit on my patio and listen to

the wind blow. I stick my Bluetooth earbuds in and listen to my screen reader play back Lady in Blue's contact information one more time. Although, I don't know why I bother — because I've played it so many times, I have it memorized.

I don't know what I'm waiting for. When did I become such a coward? I used to consider myself quite the ladies' man, but that was in my world before. Before the day which changed everything. When I went to college at Arizona State and majored in geology, I did it primarily because I loved to be outside. I used to spend all my time hiking and climbing. If I wasn't studying, I was outside exploring. That's where I met Josselyn. I thought we would be together forever, but my accident changed all that. If I couldn't fly a Huey and rescue others while earning a chest full of ribbons, she wasn't interested.

It's funny, I didn't expect her to be that kind of person because we met while I was still in college — before I started flight school with the Coast Guard. I saw lots of brass chasers when I hung out with my friends, but I never thought my wife would be of them. I was shocked she could leave me when I was at my lowest. If the shoe was on the other foot, I'm sure I would not have made the same decision. I'd like to think I would be a better person — but I'm not her.

She said the accident changed who I was. She didn't like the person I became. Words were said which couldn't be taken back. I told my wife, whom I pledged to love to my dying day, I hated the person she was too. If I had known she was such a shallow witch, I would've never married her in the first place. Well, you can't pluck those words out of the air and put them back in a bottle. It wasn't long before I received divorce papers in the mail. It was clean and simple, but not painless. I haven't spoken to Josselyn since. Everything was done through our attorneys. It was almost surgical in nature.

As I hold my phone in my hand and I listen to the Lady in Blue's phone number yet again, I wonder if so much about me has changed I am incapable of being in any sort of normal human relationship.

I'm at war with myself over these thoughts, because I remember the conversation I had with the Lady in Blue. She was eager to talk again and reluctant to hang up the phone, even under the emergency circumstances.

Finally, Derek's words float into my head and I decide to stop over thinking it and push send. I guess I should let it all go and take a few chances for a change. After all, I am on vacation.

Someone picks up the phone. "Hello?" The reception is bad and whoever is on the other end sounds like they are ill or have been on a multiple-day crying binge.

"This is John. I tried to sell you some vinyl siding the other day." I hasten to add, "Am I calling in a bad time?"

"John! I had given up on you ever calling. I thought maybe I had dreamed our whole conversation. What took you so long to call?"

"Remember the smoke alarm? They turned off the power to our building and it messed up the phone system. I wasn't able to find your phone number the usual way. I had to wait until our company produced internal productivity reports to be able to retrieve your phone number."

"Wow! I can't tell you how relieved I am to find out

it wasn't something about me. I never thought of myself as being insecure before, but it's been that kind of year for me. I guess. I feel like I'm always measuring myself against other people and coming up short. I figured that was what was happening again."

"I'm sorry I made you wait. I had no alternative. It's not as if you're listed in the phone book under 'Lady in Blue'."

"I guess that's true. I didn't give you my name or anything so you could track me down. By the way, I'm wearing yellow today if you want to change my code name."

"Nope, you will always be Lady in Blue. I envision you in a long royal blue evening gown."

She snorts on the other end of the phone. "It's clear you don't know me well, because I am the type of person who would much rather dress in torn Levi jeans — the more beat up the better — and a soft t-shirt. I love it when it gets cold enough for me to wear a worn out oversized sweatshirt with a few holes. I'm glad my uniform for work is usually scrubs — because if I had to wear a dress with pantyhose, I think I'd go nuts."

"I have to say, there aren't very many perks to being retired from the military, but not having to wear my uniform, especially my dress uniform, is one of them. I always felt like it's going to strangle me."

"I can imagine."

"So … Lady in Blue it's been a little while since I spoke to you. I guess you're still not interested in vinyl siding. Quite frankly, I'm not all that interested in selling you anything today. I'm more curious about how you are. I felt terrible about leaving you in the middle of our conversation the other day."

The pause on the other phone is so long I'm afraid my upfront approach was too in-your-face and honest. I have been out of the game far too long. I've forgotten how to flirt and be coy. Maybe I shouldn't have called at all. Perhaps I read too much into our other conversation.

When I'm about to give up and hang up, she answers my question in a quivering voice, "You don't care who I am, right? I'm a random somebody who you called on the phone." I hear her take a deep breath and then sniffle. She breathes out heavily. "Oh screw it, I've got to talk to somebody and I don't have anyone else. I hope you don't mind."

"I warn you, it's long and it's not pretty. Get comfortable. You'll be here for a while."

"Let's see, I've got a charged phone, a comfortable chair, sunscreen, and a cold beverage. I think I'm good."

I hear her chuckle a bit as she says, "Hang on, I need to refill my sweet tea and kick off my shoes and I'll be caught up with you."

"Okay, I'm not going anywhere."

I hear rustling in the background and then I hear her sigh in relief. "I don't know why I bother to wear those shoes, they kill my feet," she mumbles. "I guess I was trying to feel big and powerful today."

"What's so special about today?"

She seems to swallow a sob. "Three years ago today, I met my daughter."

"Really? Did you give her up for adoption?" I ask, trying to understand the situation.

"No, it's funny because if I had, it would've been

more socially acceptable than what I did. What I did was beyond horrible."

"I'm sorry, I'm not following," I admit.

"Have you ever made a choice in your life you thought was one hundred percent right at the time you made it, but when you look back on it, you see you were totally wrong, but you didn't know at the time?"

My mind buzzes with possibilities. I have no idea what she could mean. As I think about it, she told me she works in scrubs; so, I'm assuming she's part of the medical field. She probably had to undergo a criminal background check. So, whatever she did with her daughter, it must not have been that awful.

"I can think of several things in my life I would've done differently if I had more information," I answer vaguely.

"John, I don't even know if I want to tell you this because as weird as this sounds, I'm not as cavalier about your opinion of me as I'd like to be. I know I don't know you from Adam, but something tells me I'd probably like to."

"Blue, I've made a few stupid mistakes in my life that have had real-life consequences. I'm not in any position to be judgmental of anyone else," I reply gently. "I'm here to listen. If you want to share, that's okay. If you don't, we could talk about the weather. We'll do whatever makes you feel better. I might be old-fashioned, but I don't like to hear anybody cry. It might be because I have a little sister, but I especially don't like to hear women cry. My sister would probably kick my keister for saying that because she is a rough, tough police officer."

"I imagine she might," Lady in Blue answers. I hear

her sigh and then I hear the rattling of ice cubes as she takes a drink. "Okay, the first thing you need to know is my daughter is thirteen now. I made these decisions a long time ago when I was a different person, but it doesn't make them any more excusable. I was younger then."

"I can tell you for a fact I made completely different decisions thirteen years ago than I'd make today. You are not alone there."

"That might be true, but I doubt your decisions were quite as devastating as mine, to put it mildly, I am the world's worst mother."

"My sister has told me a lot of stories of her time in the police academy and the calls she's been on to know the definition of what passes for a mother varies greatly."

"Well, I would be on the very bottom of that list, trust me. How many mothers do you know who walk out on their children when they're toddlers?"

"More than you might imagine, actually. Even if they don't physically walk out, many of them emotionally quit."

"You know, you don't have to be this nice. I don't deserve it. I walked out on my daughter and my husband. I left them behind because I couldn't handle being a mother," she admits with a catch in her voice.

I think back to my discussions about a family with Josselyn. It was one of those things we never could quite agree on. I always wanted a big family, but Josselyn never seemed to be able to get around to it. She kept putting it off saying she wasn't ready. Of course, I didn't push her on it because I thought we would have forever together. In retrospect, I'm glad we didn't put a child through our divorce, but I don't know if Josselyn was one of those women who felt she wasn't destined to be a mother or she could foresee the end of our relationship. Because of the way our relationship crumbled, I could never ask her which it was. I wonder which is true for Blue.

"I know we don't know each other well. In fact, I don't even know your name — but, you strike me as someone who makes thoughtful, careful decisions. I suspect if you left your daughter and husband behind, there had to be an outside force involved. Was your husband hurting you?"

"No!" she insists. "Or, at least not intentionally. Toward the end, I think we were hurting each other simply because we were young and didn't know what else to do in our situation."

"What situation?" I ask, dreading the answer. I feel like I'm holding my breath. I want to hear the whole explanation, but I'm almost afraid of what I'll find out. I have a fantasy of what my Lady in Blue is like in my mind, and I don't want that to be shattered. On the other hand, I love the fact she's so real and candid.

"Well, Mark and I married for all the wrong reasons. We grew up together. Our parents had known each other for ages and we married to make them happy. We didn't know what marriage was like, we only knew what it was like in the movies and on TV. Even though we were friends, we knew nothing about each other on an intimate level. We didn't know how to live together; we didn't even have common goals."

I shift in my chair and let out a deep breath. This isn't so bad.

"Mark was one of those people who excelled at

everything he did. But he didn't want anybody to know. In high school, he took college courses but didn't even tell anyone. He wanted to fit in with everyone else."

"I know people like that," I comment.

"Yeah, me too. Anyway, I was a few years younger than Mark, but my parents didn't care because they had watched him grow up. We didn't plan to get pregnant. We were trying to prevent it, but I got pregnant anyway. Mark had just started law school. It was a crazy time. At first, after I got over the shock, I was happy. I thought having a baby might make us more like a regular married couple instead of two friends pretending to play house. I figured it might make me feel like more of a grown-up. Instead, I was dreadfully sick my whole pregnancy. Everyone told me I would feel better after my first trimester, but I never did. I was already feeling like a huge failure because I had to be hospitalized twice during my pregnancy because I was so dehydrated from throwing up."

"From what I understand, that's not unusual. Isn't there a medical condition related to that?"

"Yes, it's called *hyperemesis gravidarum*. I know that now, but I had no idea about it back then. I thought I was just a failure for not being able to support my baby properly."

"I'm sorry. That shouldn't have been your burden."

"Thank you for saying that," she whispers. "But there's so much more to my story."

"It's all right, take your time."

"When we brought Ketki home, she developed jaundice and then she got colic, I thought both of those things were my fault. She never stopped crying, and soon I couldn't either."

"That's rough," I murmur.

"You have no idea. I tried to breastfeed and I couldn't do that either. I felt like there was nothing related to motherhood I could do correctly. My baby screamed all the time. I couldn't even touch her without her breaking out in a new round of crying. There was nothing I could do to console her or make her happy. She lost weight and trembled every time I came near."

Blue sighs and I hear her take a long drink. I can count her swallows.

"This is so humiliating for me to even tell you, but I told you I would tell you the whole story, so here goes."

"There's nothing to be humiliated about. It sounds like the whole deck of cards was stacked against you."

"That's kind of you to say, but I stacked a lot of those cards myself. Poor Mark. I don't even know how he finished law school. I basically gave up on life. I stopped showering, brushing my teeth, cooking, or taking care of Ki. I couldn't make myself get out of bed."

"Sounds incredibly difficult," I commiserate. Although I'm not ready to share my story yet, after I lost my vision, I had many days where I didn't get out of my bed. I couldn't find the strength to face the challenges of my day.

"It was. My daughter and my husband were the ones who paid the price. If it had only been lethargy, I probably would've stayed and worked through it, but I started to have dark thoughts."

"What do you mean? Like suicidal thoughts?" I cringe when I consider that idea. I've been there and done that too.

"Sometimes, but it was worse than that. So much

worse."

I hold my breath as I consider the implications of her statement.

Her voice lowers to a whisper. "Sometimes when I was feeling particularly awful, I would begin to wonder what life would be like if I didn't have Ki — like if she didn't exist at all. I started to think about ways to get rid of her."

"Whoa! Heavy stuff. What did your husband say?"

"Nothing. I didn't tell him. He was in law school and struggling to keep up with his classes while taking care of Ki. I didn't want to add one more thing. I thought I was going absolutely crazy."

"I can imagine why you would feel that way, but he was your friend at least. Wouldn't he have done something?"

"Oh, I'm sure he would've. Mark is the consummate problem solver. It's what he does. He is an extraordinary human being. I wasn't in a mental state where I could admit I had any problems at all. I already felt like a total failure and I didn't want to show anybody any weakness."

"As former military, I can understand that feeling."

"Besides, Mark had bigger problems with Ki. He always knew something was going on with her, and if I had been a little less absorbed with my problems, I probably would've picked up on it too. I thought she hated me."

"Picked up on what?" I feel like I missed part of the conversation.

"Ketki is autistic. Once Mark got her diagnosis, I knew he would throw all his energy into trying to make her better. So, I knew whatever the heck was wrong with me, I had to figure it out on my own and stay out of Mark's way."

"What a jerk!" I exclaim.

"I know, it was terrible of me. I walked out on them both. I felt like the scum of the earth."

"No, I don't mean you. I mean *him*," I hurry to explain. "He should have seen something was going on with you and helped you."

"No, that's not what this is about. Remember, I told you we were both incredibly young and had no business being married? Mark was going crazy trying to balance it all and I wasn't pulling my own weight. He was working, taking care of Ketki and going to school. Top it all off, I dumped it all in his lap."

"I know you haven't convinced your heart it's not your fault, but when did you convince your brain?" I ask as all the pieces of the puzzle fall into place.

Blue gasps. "How could you possibly know? I barely told you anything about my life."

"I just started putting the shards of information together. You said you work in scrubs. I figure you must be in the medical field. You also said this happened when you were young. Therefore, you must've pursued the medical career after you left your marriage. I'm making assumptions based on what I would do if it were me. I suspect that I would go searching for answers. I'm guessing you studied everything there is to know about postpartum depression and autism and maybe even genetics."

"How did you even put it together with postpartum depression? Most people don't even know about that."

"I had a buddy in flight school whose wife had to be hospitalized for postpartum psychosis. It was a traumatic thing for everyone involved. He didn't know about it either until it happened to his wife."

"Yeah, psychotic is a good term for how I felt," she admits. "I'll never forget that day as long as I live. I felt like if I didn't leave, I would hurt Ketki or myself."

"So, I guess what I don't understand is why you think I would blame you for a medical condition that's not your fault? I'm not judging you."

"But … if I had told people what was going on and admitted I was having trouble dealing with my life, maybe I could have handled things better and stayed in my daughter's life. Maybe I gave up too easily."

"Maybe you didn't. Maybe you saved your daughter's life and your own. Remember how you prefaced this conversation with me? You said you made decisions based on the information you had at the time. You didn't know any better. You did the best you could. How can I fault you for that?"

"John, I know you mean well and you've said all the right things. I want you to take a couple days to think about the fact I thought about killing my daughter at some point in my life. Think about what kind of person that makes me and decide whether you ever want to talk to me again. If you do, call me back."

"Blue, you are being way too hard on yourself. You don't need to take the blame for this. It was a chemical imbalance in your brain, not a character deficit."

"John, someone else is raising my daughter and is married to the man who was once my husband because of the decisions I made. Do you get that? I walked away because I wanted to destroy all I had. I can't help but wonder if there is still some evil left in me. So, think about that for a couple days."

"I will. I don't think it'll change my mind. There's something my life has taught me. Sometimes, courage looks different from what you might expect. Sweet Dreams, Blue. I'll talk to you later."

"Good night, John. Thanks for calling. I needed to tell my story. I'm so grateful you were willing to listen."

# CHAPTER FIVE

# TAYANITA

MARIO'S BUON APPETITO. NOTHING like having to face down my fears and resist delicious food at the same time. At first I wondered if maybe I misinterpreted the text message, then I see Ketki hunched over a menu.

"Oh good, you're here! I couldn't decide whether you would want the three-tomato pizza or the pizza with salami. I've seen you eat both. I was going to order ahead because I'm starving; but I couldn't figure out which one you would like the most."

Taking my seat at the table and putting my purse down by my feet, I answer, "Usually when I'm stuck, I order half-and-half."

Ketki wrinkles her nose at me as she answers, "You can't have two types of pizza touch each other. That's gross."

"That's okay, I don't mind. I'll eat the slices where they touch."

"You can eat four pieces of pizza?" My daughter has a look of shock on her face.

I shrug. "I skipped breakfast. If you order a medium pizza, it's not so much."

"Wow! Dad says Shelby and I eat a lot. He should be glad he's not feeding *you*." She giggles.

After I place her order with the perky waitress, I turn to Ketki and ask, "So, what's up with all the cloak and dagger stuff? Why are we having pizza in the middle of the afternoon on a Saturday? Where's your dad?"

Ketki rolls her eyes at me. "You are as bad as they are." She pulls up her sleeve and shows me a fancy watch. "See? I'm being monitored by GPS. They know where I am. I promise I'm not a runaway. Geez, I'm thirteen years old. I should be able to go to the local strip mall and have dinner with my mom."

"Okay, so you've established you are not on the lam, but that doesn't explain why you and I are having lunch," I press.

"I called you to see if you are still mad at me," explains Ketki.

"I was never mad at you."

"You were mad at my birthday party. I saw your face. You were so angry you had to leave. Dad didn't notice because he was too busy kissing Shelby, but I saw you. You looked like I feel when the kids are bullying me at school. I know you were very upset. I figured you were pissed off at me and you didn't want to tell me."

Her words are like daggers to my heart. I hadn't even realized she was paying any attention on her birthday. I thought Mark and Shelby were keeping her busy with video games. I knew she was sad to see me go, but I didn't realize she had taken it so personally.

"Ketki, you have it all wrong. It wasn't about you. Really."

"Are you sure? It sure seemed like it was," she

challenges.

"Okay, so I said that wrong. It was about you. It was all about you, but not in the way you think."

Ketki looks crestfallen. Instinctively, I reach out to grab her hand. She yanks it back and I am once again reminded that she doesn't like to be touched. I forge ahead with my explanation anyway.

"Ketki, your birthday was incredibly hard for me. You are becoming such a beautiful young woman and that day was a stark reminder to me of all the things I've lost out on by not being part of your life."

A myriad of emotions crosses her face before she blurts, "Dad's not here, so I'm gonna say it — well duh. I'm sorry, Tayanita. What did you expect? I couldn't stay like a little baby forever. I had to grow up whether you were there or not. I'm not a baby doll you could set down when you were bored with me."

Ketki's words feel like a direct blow. But it's nothing I haven't said to myself a million times. Most days at work, I keep myself busy enough that I don't have time to think about it. But it's at night at home alone in my house when thoughts creep in about who I should have been, who I wanted to be if I had been a better person, if I had been stronger … if I had been the mother I always dreamed of being. My reality is I'm not that person. I'm just me; the person who epically failed Ketki.

"Actually, I'm surprised you haven't said that before. It's a fair criticism. I deserve it. It hurts, but it's not untrue," I reason, trying to keep my voice even and unemotional. I'm not sure I meet my goal. At least I'm *trying* not to upset her further. Something tells me it's a little too late as she looks at me and shakes her head.

"Shelby has tried to explain this to me. She tells me I'm not supposed to be ugly to you. I know it's not your fault, like autism is not my fault. Most of the time, I get that. Some days, our bodies make us do things we don't want them to do. But sometimes, I still get mad you're not around. I forget it's not because you don't care."

A tear escapes my eye and rolls down my cheek. "Ketki, please understand it was never, ever because I didn't care. I left *because* I cared. I wanted the best for you. I knew I would never be good for you. It's like the mom part of me is broken and I didn't know how to fix it. I was afraid if I stayed my depression might cause me to do something to hurt you. I couldn't make my thoughts turn around and make any sense. I knew Mark would take good care of you. I figured if he didn't have me to worry about, he could focus on your needs."

"*Etsi,* that's silly. Daddy always loved you even when you weren't around."

My heart about stops in my chest when I hear her refer to me as 'mother' in Cherokee. It's the first time I've ever heard her call me anything other than Tayanita or Nita.

Collecting myself, I look sharply at Ketki and ask in a hoarse whisper, "How do you know this?"

Ketki rolls her shoulder in my direction. "It was kind of obvious. He waited for you to come back forever. It was like he finally gave up after my uncle died. I never saw him so sad. It was like he gave up hope."

I lean my head back against the vinyl booth and close my eyes as I remember the vibrant eccentric artist who used to be Mark's younger brother. He used to tease me all the time growing up about my friendship with his big brother. Callum was furious with me when I left. I ran into him once at the bank and he let me have it with both barrels. It was enough to reduce me to tears in front of the whole bank. It's particularly sad to me that Callum never got to see me reunite with Ketki.

"Ki, I think you must've misunderstood, because your dad always knew how to reach me, but he never did."

"No, I understand everything. You know dad. He would never admit his feelings were hurt. He would do the British thing — you know stiff upper lip and all that. I never saw him show he needed anybody besides the two of us until he met Shelby. He tried to pretend everything was fine even though I knew we weren't a normal family. He was always waiting for something to happen."

"He waited all those years for me to come back?"

"Yeah, he did. For somebody who's so book-smart, sometimes my dad can't catch a clue. Grandma and Grandpa even tried to play matchmaker, but he wouldn't listen to them."

"What did you think of all of this?" I ask, feeling curious about her reaction.

"I didn't know what to think. For a while, I tried to help. I tried to match Dad up with various people, like my teacher, the mail lady, and the choir teacher at church. I didn't understand the rules of the game. Some of those people were already married to other people. Dad finally asked me to stop. So, I did. I decided the two of us were a team and we didn't need anyone else."

"What did you think happened to me?" I ask before I can stop myself. I suck in a breath because I'm not sure I want to know the answer to this question. My brain got ahead of my common sense and now the question is hanging out there waiting to be answered. I don't know what Mark told Ketki about me. He could have made me out to be a witch, and I would've deserved every second of that reputation.

Ketki's gaze skitters away from me again. I brace for the worst. Ketki straightens in her seat. She takes a bite of pizza and a long drink of soda before she recalls with a bemused expression, "Dad would always get a silly smile on his face before he would tell me you were the person who taught him what it meant to give up everything you had to love with your whole heart. You loved us both so much you gave up everything to keep us safe. He said you would forever be his first love."

I suck in a deep breath as I hear those words because that's not what I expected my daughter to say. "Honestly? That's what he told you about me? I figured he would be furious with me and say much worse about me."

"Well, he did say a few more things," Ketki discloses.

"Yeah? Like what?" I ask, waiting for the other shoe to drop.

"Daddy says I'm beautiful like you. He also said he hopes I grow up to be smart like you."

"Okay, now I know you're making it up! Your dad is the smart one in the family."

"Says the surgical nurse," responds Ketki pointedly.

"I am now; but I wasn't when I was with your dad. I had just started CNA classes."

"Yeah, I know. But Daddy said you were acing them like nobody's business. He said you progressed through the classes super fast. He also said the clients totally loved you."

"I wish I would have been able to listen to how proud Mark was of me back then, but I couldn't hear what he was saying. I could only see what I wasn't doing right."

"Maybe what you had was a little like my autism. Sometimes, it feels like I have too many things competing for attention in my brain. Maybe whatever it was that caused you to have the bad feelings about yourself drowned out all the good things."

"That's a good description of what happened. It really did feel like I was drowning. I couldn't catch my breath. I couldn't tell which end was up in my life, but it didn't have anything to do with you or your dad. It was all about me. You two were my favorite people in the entire world."

"I believe you, but I have one question," Ketki asks as she studies me intently.

I nod as I say, "Go ahead, I have no secrets."

"I changed my mind, I have two questions."

I grin. "Are you sure?"

"Never mind, I always have more questions than that."

"I'm ready whenever you are," I answer as I take a couple of bites of pizza.

"So, the thing that's always bugged me since I figured out who you are is that you got well enough to go to nursing school and get a big important job, right?"

I nod slowly as I chew.

"That took some time, didn't it?"

"It did."

"If you weren't drowning anymore why didn't you

come back to Daddy? He still loved you and I was still alone."

There it is; the question that has haunted me for years. It wasn't so much why I left. I left in a moment of crisis. To a certain extent, it was understandable. In retrospect, if I'd sought proper treatment for my postpartum depression, it would've probably been diagnosed as postpartum psychosis. The behavior I have a harder time explaining to myself or anyone else is why I stayed away even after I got healthy.

Now, I am face-to-face with my thirteen-year-old daughter and she is asking me for an explanation. I swallow hard and take a drink of my soda before I admit softly, "I was scared and deeply ashamed."

"Scared of what?" Ketki asks.

"I was scared you wouldn't know who I was or that your dad moved on and had fallen out of love with me. I was afraid he would hate me for my choice and he wouldn't understand why I did what I did."

"Didn't you try to talk to Dad the whole time you were gone? I thought you loved Daddy."

"Ki, I did love him. But I wasn't making very clear-headed decisions when it came to my personal life back then. I was pushing him away, but expecting him to chase after me at the same time. I know that doesn't make any sense to you right now — in fact, it might not ever make sense. Still, that's the kind of mess I stuck your Dad in. I'm not proud of it and that's why I don't blame him for the decisions we made together. We both did the best we could under the circumstances. Your dad has done a phenomenal job with you. I'm so proud of who you have become."

"I thought you were ashamed of me. I think Daddy thought you hated him too."

It's all I can do not to drop my jaw on the ground in shock. But I didn't leave her an alternative storyline. As a teenager, I suspect I would've come to the same conclusions. "Ketki, I'm so sorry. I never meant for you to feel that way. I've never hated you, not even for one second."

I squeeze my eyes shut, trying to hold back the memories. I grimace as I admit candidly, "I've never hated your dad either. Sometimes, my feelings were hurt because we couldn't make things work out between us, but I've never hated him. It's hard, for me to watch him be so happy with Shelby and realize I gave all that up. Even so, I've never disliked him and I've done nothing but love you with my whole heart."

"So, you didn't leave because I have autism?" she asks again.

"No! I didn't leave because you have autism. I left because I wasn't strong enough to help you with your disability. I had too many issues in my own life. I didn't know it at the time, but my own postpartum depression was taking over my life and I couldn't think clearly."

"This isn't about you being embarrassed?" Ketki presses.

"Of course not. If anything, it's about me being ashamed of *me*. I could never be ashamed of you. You are phenomenal," I insist. "Why would you think I would leave because I was embarrassed?" I'm curious to see if there's anything behind her insistent question.

Ketki shrugs and diverts her gaze as she asks, "Well, I'm not sure how much to believe the kids at my school, you know what I mean?"

I shake my head slightly, "I'm not sure I understand. Why don't you explain to me what's going on?"

"I don't know. It seems a little stupid, but I didn't know what to think."

"There aren't any dumb questions, you know," I encourage.

"Okay, there's this one popular girl in my class. Her name is Jordyn with a Y. She always tells people about the Y. I think it's kind of bizarre, but whatever. Anyway, she told me the reason you never stuck around was because you were embarrassed to be seen with me because I'm so weird and the only reason Dad hangs around me is because he has to or he'll go to jail."

"For the record, Jordyn with a Y needs to get a life. She has no business poking around in yours. Secondly, what she said is totally not true."

"*Etsi,* now you're lying. I am weird. Autism makes me different, you know that."

"*Agehuts*, you're right. I am not going to sugarcoat it. Autism does make things harder, but it doesn't make you unlovable. It makes you different. In some ways, different is cool. Like how you know tons about computers and not everyone is like that."

"But what about the rest?"

"The rest was because I was sick. It had nothing to do with you."

"Then why do you hate yourself so much?" Ketki asks in a steady voice. "If you're not mad at me for having autism, why are you mad at yourself for having postpartum depression?"

## Mary Crawford

It's such a simple question. I'm not sure why it's taken me a lifetime and an advanced degree in the medical field to figure it out.

# CHAPTER SIX

# JOHN

I BREATHE A SIGH of relief when the Lady in Blue answers her phone. I've been trying for days to reach her. I even went as far as having Derek check her number on my phone to verify nothing had altered it. I began to second-guess myself when all I received was a weird mechanical voice instructing me to leave a message. Unlike most people, Blue has elected not to leave any personal clues behind on her voicemail about her identity.

I debated long and hard about what kind of message to leave her. In the end, I decide not to leave any voice mail. Given the tenor of our last conversation, nothing seemed appropriate. Blue was so convinced I would never call back after she shared her personal story with me. I simply couldn't determine the appropriate approach. Cutesy and light seemed disrespectful to the experience we shared together and leaving a perfunctory and business-like message would make it seem like I totally disregarded the whole emotional impact of what we have been through. So, I waited until I could talk to her in person. Now that the moment is upon me, I have to take a moment to collect myself before I can speak.

"Good evening, Lady in Blue. For the record, just

because you dodge my calls, doesn't mean I haven't been trying to reach you."

A tingle goes up my spine as she chuckles in her special husky tone. "John, you don't understand how much I needed to hear from you today."

"I'm glad to hear that. I'm only a phone call away if you need to talk. You know, phone lines go both ways."

I can hear her sigh. "I know, and it probably seems like I am trying to avoid your phone calls, but that's not what's happening here, I promise. Fate seems to be conspiring against me having an actual life."

"It sounds like there's a story there. I'm all ears if you want to grab a glass of wine, or something stronger, and tell me all about it," I offer.

Blue groans. "You have no idea how tempting that offer is. But I'm so tired if I even so much as smell alcohol at this point I'm probably going to completely pass out. So, I'll have to settle for something as disgustingly healthy as orange juice."

"Hey, healthy is good. I won't knock you for that," I answer as I sip my coffee. "On the other hand, I'm probably not going to confess to you I am drinking coffee with four shots of espresso and enough sugar to keep an army of dentists employed. Oops, I guess I probably just did."

"Don't look at me. Today I want to forget I'm a nurse. Think of me as a Rockette or something."

"Works for me!" I answer with a loud laugh. "I've always been a bit of a leg man."

Lady in Blue snorts inelegantly. "Let me guess, you're also a boob man?"

"Not as much as I once was in my younger days," I confess candidly.

"Well, I can't tell you how relieved that makes me. You wouldn't believe the number of surgeries I assist with where the women are altering themselves to make the men in their lives happy. It's a sad commentary on life. I have to bite my tongue a lot in my job to keep from speaking out. The plastic surgeons I work for make a lot of money making men's fantasies come true. It's not my job to share my moral commentary on how they make money. I need to shut up and do my job."

"That must be awkward. It must be a little like being in the military and disagreeing with orders. You're not at liberty to say anything even when you see the mission headed toward a train wreck."

"Exactly!" Blue exclaims. "Sometimes before anesthesia, these women take medication to help them relax and they end up telling me the whole story. I want to shake them and tell them they are beautiful without surgery, but I can't without risking my job."

"But if something was life-and-death, you have the freedom to bring it up, right?" I ask.

"Oh absolutely. If something were amiss with the patient, I would be waving red flags all over the place. In fact, I have a reputation for being a bit of a stick-in-the-mud — a stickler for procedure."

I chuckle softly. "Oh, I see. You're one of those; I guess every team has to have one."

Blue sighs. "It's all right, you can hate me. I know most everyone else does. I'm commonly known as Witch Central on my team. That's why I was surprised when I was recently promoted. Maybe it pays to be picky sometimes. Unfortunately, it may not matter how good I am at my job."

Something about her tone alerts me to the fact this is the big topic we've been talking around for a while. "So this is it? The thing we're not talking about, but really talking about when we're not talking about it?"

I hear her take a large gulp of her drink before she finally says, "Yeah, I guess we are. Not talking about it and pretending it's not happening isn't helping me. It's not like I have anyone else to confess this to. So, if you're up to this, I guess I'll share with you. But, I still haven't figured out why you want to know my deepest, darkest secrets. It's not even as if you're my friend."

"Lady in Blue, I don't think that's true. We might not have met in the most conventional of ways, but I've shared things with you most people don't know about me and I know sides of you that you don't show to anyone else. I think that makes us friends of sorts."

"Well, you probably should know my name if I'm going to tell you something as big as this."

"I would love to know what to call you, but it's not necessary unless you want to tell me. I'm as happy to call you Blue if it will make you feel comfortable."

"John, I passed comfortable with you a long time ago. If I hadn't been comfortable with you, I wouldn't have told you half of the things I've shared."

"True. Our conversations have been a little on the candid side."

"Okay, for the sake of honesty, my name is Tayanita. A lot of folks find it easier to call me Nita."

I try her name out. "It's nice to formally meet you, Tayanita. Something told me you would have a beautiful exotic name. I couldn't see you having an ordinary name like Mary or Sue."

"I know, it's a weird name. No customized novelties for me. You can call me Nita if it makes you feel more comfortable. I'm used to it."

"I never said your name was weird," I protest. "I think it's beautiful. I meant I pictured you as someone unusual and exotic in my mind. A simple name like Mary or Sue would not fit you. Now that we're on a first-name basis, what's this other deep, dark secret weighing you down?"

"I don't know if I should share this with you, all the secret sharing seems to be one-sided here — what about you? What are your deep dark secrets?"

"I've already told you I'm not thrilled with my job. My little sister's job scares the crap out of me and I'm an epic failure as a husband. I think I've spilled a number of secrets."

"True enough," Tayanita concedes. "Those seem like little secrets compared to what I have to tell you. I've never actually said this out loud while I was sober but there is no simple way to say it other than to come out and say the words."

"I think telling hard truths is like taking bad tasting medicine, you have to do it and get it over with. Once it's done, it will be easier to cope with," I advise. "However hard it is, I'm here for you."

"As silly as it seems, you'll never know how much I appreciate that, John. You know, I've known from the time I became a CNA all those years ago, working in the world of healthcare carried risks. Still, I figured it would be from something like pinkeye or maybe a repeated severe case of the flu from being exposed to patients all the time. I never thought it would be from HIV. I'm meticulous about following protocol. I drill it into my interns all the time. This patient, according to his records, was not even supposed to be positive."

"Oh no — what happened, Blue? Needle stick?"

"No, it couldn't even be that cliché. I managed to get splashed in the face from a femoral bleed. I couldn't get my face shield up in time."

"Well, I guess if there's a good way to be exposed that's probably it. Low risk of transmission."

"So they tell me."

"It's true. The incidence is low and the treatability is exceptionally high. I'm assuming you've already taken your first set of labs?"

"Yeah, I had blood tests immediately after the hospital was notified of the patient's HIV status. To be honest, I'm having a hard time knowing what to believe about all of this. The Risk Management folks tell me the chances of me developing AIDS is slim, but it's in their best interest to tell me that too. Statistically, I know it's low. Then again, technically speaking, he should have never gotten in my operating room without us knowing he was HIV-positive to begin with, and the chances of a femoral bleed shooting me directly in the face with my years of experience as a surgical nurse was next to none. Yet it happened. So, you want to tell me again about those odds?"

"Tayanita I'm not a person to lecture you about odds. I've seen more than my fair share of difficult odds in my life, and been beat by them. If the fates had been kinder to me, I wouldn't be trying to sell you vinyl siding in a sweat box of an office in a job I absolutely detest."

"Why is it you are working in a job you hate? Clearly you have the brains to do much more. If I didn't know better, I'd say you might actually be somebody from my field. You seem to know all about the risks I faced from my patient."

"I bet you were killer at twenty questions, Blue," I tease in an attempt to stall. Even as the words escape, I realize I'm not being fair. I clear my throat and start again. "You're right. I know those things because I am former military. I was a Coastie as they say. I flew the helicopter on rescue missions. I worked with flight nurses and paramedics every day. I even went through advanced EMT training so I would know how to help render aid when we were on the ground. So, I know the risks you face as a nurse."

"Former?" she asks abruptly, "From what I know of military guys, it's not something you quit being."

"That's a true statement if I've ever heard one," I remark.

"Were you forced out by some scandal? Let me guess ... is it something juicy related to one of your other secrets? Are you an epic failure as a husband because you were sleeping with your commander's wife?"

I let loose with a surprised hoot of laughter. "No! I like my nuts right where they are, thank you very much."

"Hmm ... maybe you played so much poker you became a double agent and got busted for espionage."

"Bite your tongue, woman. I am no spy. I play poker but only for cigarette money."

"John, I know I said I wouldn't play nurse tonight, but cigarette money ... yuck! Talk about your poor life choices."

"Trust me, you're preaching to the choir. That's a life choice that's in my past like my service in the military. I left cigarettes behind."

"I can't tell you how relieved I am to hear you say you don't smoke anymore. I can't stand to kiss an ashtray."

"Kissing? I don't recall ever talking about kissing — although I much prefer to talk about kissing rather than my failed military career. In fact, we can talk about kissing all day. How do you like to kiss?" I ask lightly.

Tayanita lets out a breath of exasperation. "I'm not sure we are at a point where that's any of your business. You know I didn't mean it that way. I was trying to be supportive of your decision not to smoke. I'd like to know more about what led to your decision to leave your career in the military."

"It would probably be easier to take if it was my decision to leave. But it wasn't. It was all the result of something stupid. I let my ego get ahead of my common sense and I hurt a bunch of people who didn't deserve to pay the price, including me. It was one of those occasions in which I came out on the losing end of fate." I stop and think for a moment, lost in terrible memories. "Come to think of it, depending on how you view the situation, I was either the luckiest son of a gun on the planet or one of the unluckiest. I'm still coming to terms with that. I lost all my sense of identity. That's part of the reason I was on the other end of the phone selling you vinyl siding. As much as I hate that god-awful job, I can't regret the fact that it brought us together."

I hear Tayanita shift the phone on her shoulder and sigh. "I know what you mean. If I hadn't needed a friend so much that particular day, I would've slammed the phone down in your ear without so much as a polite 'no thank you' and never said another word to you. I might've lost the chance to make one of the strongest connections I've made with another human in a long time. It's funny how fate gives us a chance to rectify our pasts."

# Chapter Seven

# Tayanita

I WAIT UNTIL I am in the privacy of the bathroom stall to open the envelope marked confidential. I was offered counseling before receiving this news, but I elected to turn it down. Now as I run my thumbnail under the flap of the envelope, I wonder if I made a foolish decision.

My mom always did say I have a stupidly large amount of pride, but I can't see myself falling apart in front of a bunch of coworkers and having it get back to anyone I know. I know all about confidentiality rules and professional ethics and all that. I also know how things go around the back halls of the hospital. The rumor mill runs wild in a hospital even when it shouldn't. I don't need anything to undermine my professional reputation especially when I am new to the role of supervisor. I have to appear strong and invincible to the people who work for me.

I take a deep breath and will my hands to hold still as I open the letter containing the lab results. I let out the breath I am holding as I decipher the various values. It is difficult for me to see through my tears, but as I blink them away, it becomes increasingly clear things seem to be going in my favor for once.

My markers are negative for HIV.

I know I won't truly be in the clear for several more months. But, this is a start.

I glance at my watch and realize John should be off work in a few minutes. I pull out my cell phone and dial his number.

"Blue? Is everything okay?" he greets automatically with concern in his voice.

"See? That's exactly why I'm calling. I always call you with doom and gloom. I'm calling because I want to celebrate. I have spectacular news and I want to go out and have a good time. I want to party. Do you want to join me?"

"I'm afraid you might find my method of celebrating a lot different from what you expect," John admits with a sigh. "Actually, you would probably find a lot about me surprising if you met me in person."

"Oh … umm … you're not one of those guys who have seven or eight wives stashed in a mansion somewhere, are you?" I ask feeling a little silly about my impromptu invitation.

John laughs in his deep rich laugh. "No, I definitely do not have multiple wives. I do not have any wives much to the dismay of my mother. My mother considers it a personal affront to her matchmaking ability that I am currently single."

"You're not one of those people who collect belly button lint or earwax, are you?"

"No! Definitely not. I went to basic training with one of those — he was beyond disgusting. I'm not your typical guy. I never was the type of guy who liked to go dancing in clubs or out to fancy restaurants. I prefer going camping and hiking to any of the traditional stuff."

"John, if I didn't know better, I'd say you've done some background digging on me. One of the reasons I find it hard to date is because I'm kind of more like a guy than a traditional girl. I love being out in nature but I also like working on cars and playing video games. Playing video games was actually how I met Ketki face-to-face a few years ago. We share that passion."

"That's cool, actually."

"Most guys think it's cool until they expect me to act like a regular woman and I don't quite know how to fill that role."

"You and I haven't done anything by the book. Nothing says we have to start now."

"Okay, let's say I buy that premise. What do you say to dinner out at the hiking trails? I'll bring dinner from the deli and my camera. We can take some great sunset shots."

John groans. "Oh my Gosh. You know how to throw a low blow. That is one of my favorite places in all of Florida. I would love to go."

"Great, text me your address and I'll pick you up in about forty-five minutes. You don't have anything against me driving, do you? I got a new rig when I got my promotion and I haven't driven it much for fun."

"I don't mind if you drive. In fact —"

"Oh shoot! Ketki's calling. I'll see you in a bit," I say as my phone beeps.

"Wait … Tayanita I need to tell you something —" John blurts in a rush.

"Tell me later. I'll be seeing you in a few minutes

anyway. We'll talk about it then. Dress in layers, it can get windy out there."

I click my phone over to Ketki.

"Hey, Ki, what's up?" I ask, a little breathless.

"Are you okay, *Etsi?* You sound weird. This isn't about the whole dying thing, is it?"

"No, it's not. But, how do you even know about that?"

"I heard Aunt Savannah ask Shelby about it when they didn't realize I was in the hallway. I wasn't eavesdropping on purpose, I swear. I left my room to go to the bathroom and accidentally overheard their conversation. It was interesting because Aunt Savannah was asking about statistics and odds. You know how I like math."

"Yes, I know. But you don't need to worry. I got my comprehensive results back and I don't have the antibody. My test came back negative."

"Then why do you sound so weird?"

"If you must know, Ms. Nosy Pants, I think I might have a kind of, sort of, date tonight."

"That would probably make me sound weird too."

"Um-hmm, I'm a little nervous. To be honest, it's been a long time since I've done anything like this. What if he takes one look at me and decides I'm nothing like he thought I'd be?"

"You're silly. Aren't you always the one who tells me we shouldn't judge people by the way they look or dress?"

"I suppose I am. Not everyone plays by the same rules. I'm not even sure what this guy looks like. We haven't talked about it much. He used to be in the military. So, I suppose he's in good shape."

I can almost hear my daughter roll her eyes at me as she responds, "So are you. Didn't you run the half marathon a couple of months ago?"

"Okay, fine so jogging is a good stress reliever from work. A lot of people run for fun."

"I don't think I know anybody who runs as much as you do," Ketki responds. "Anyway, all the magazines I read say to be yourself on the first date and be nice and complimentary to your date. Everything should be fine. Be sure to call Mom and let her know who you're with and where you're going. That's basic dating safety and still applies to you even though you're a grown up."

"Thanks, Ketki. Did you call for a reason?"

"Yeah, we're selling candy bars and jerky for my class at school. Would you mind taking some to your break room at work and seeing if people will buy some? You know how I hate going door-to-door to sell stuff."

"You couldn't get Tristan to sell out of his company lunchroom this year?"

"Yeah, he's going to sell it there too. But, the most popular girl in class is having her dad sell it at a golf retreat and honestly I'd like to sell more than her."

"Sounds like a fabulous plan."

"*Esti?* Be nice to this guy. He's way more nervous than you. He's feeling kind of lost in the world," Ketki mumbles.

"How do you know, Ki? You don't even know who I'm going out with."

"Sometimes I have strong hunches about stuff."

As I am driving up to John's house, I carefully listen to the weird voice coming from my phone giving me ever so precise directions. I'm trying to calm my jitters. Usually, I'm better at disguising my nerves than this. I actually have sweat on the back of my neck. I don't think I've been this nervous since Mark took me to his junior prom.

I lift the heavy knocker and knock on the door. I notice my fingers are trembling. *Get it together Taya, you're going on a dinner hike, not an international spy mission.* As soon as I have that thought, I jump about a mile and a half in the air when John's voice comes through a small intercom beside the door.

"Tayanita, you're a little earlier than I expected. Please let yourself in. I hope you're not allergic to cats. Corkscrew is very friendly. He likes to serve as my welcoming committee. I'll be right with you. Make yourself at home."

It's been a while since I've done a lot of dating, but I have gone out a few times and this is the most unorthodox greeting I've received in a while. Maybe I'm reading way too much into this whole situation. I carefully open the door and peek inside.

Although not as modern and sleek as some doctors' houses I have visited, everything is compulsively neat. There isn't anything out of place. Even the throw pillows on the couch are lined up perfectly straight. I instinctively straighten my spine and fix my purse strap. I carefully make my way over to a leather couch and perch on the very edge, for fear I might mess up the rigid perfection. Suddenly, from over my shoulder, an orange ball of fluff plops into my lap with a surprised meow. Whoever came up with the theory that cats always land on their feet never met this little one. He face-plants into my thigh. He gets up and shakes his head as if to clear out any stars and confusion — like a cartoon character. He looks up at me with big blue eyes and purrs. He tries to rub up against my purse which is sitting next to me on the couch but he loses his balance and falls over.

"I hate to tell you this John, but I think your kitty has been hitting the catnip a little hard. He's having trouble keeping his balance."

John explains from the other room, "No, that's just Corkscrew. My sister rescued him on a domestic violence call. The dirtbag of a husband was abusing him to torture the wife. So, he has the equivalent of a traumatic brain injury. They don't know if he will ever get better. There is more than one reason he's called Corkscrew."

At the moment, the kitten is trying to climb my arm to get to my earring. "I can't believe anybody would try to hurt this little thing. He is so cute. I can't help but hope the bad guy got what was coming to him."

"Katie never said anything, but I was told he had a nice little goose egg on his head in his booking photo. It is possible she forgot to tell the perp to duck before he got in the squad car."

"That's the least he deserves for hurting this baby," I ask as I stroke his fragile body. "How did you end up with him?"

"Remember I told you my mom is anxious to get me married off again? Well, she read an article that stated men who have pets are more likely to find mates so she figured Corkscrew would be the perfect 'chick bait' as she put it."

I laugh out loud. "Well, I can't argue with her there. He's very effective. I'm finding it hard to resist his adorableness. That also sounds like something my family would do. I'm surprised they haven't thought of it. My mom still hasn't forgiven me for letting Mark get away."

Corkscrew is busy trying to climb my shirt and curl up in the crook of my neck. It's been a while since I've been around small kittens. I've forgotten how sharp their little claws are. I wasn't paying attention to my surroundings until from behind me I hear an odd clicking sound. My heart races and the hairs on my arms stand up as I realize what a vulnerable position I'm in. Ketki's safe dating tips ring loud in my ears. Blowing out the breath I've been holding, I slowly turn around to face John.

"I can't tell you how happy my mom would be to hear all of her strategizing isn't going to waste," John says with a smile.

At least, that's what I think he said. To be honest, my brain isn't focusing on his words at all. Instead, it's working on solving the puzzle I see before me.

That strange clicking sound I heard? It wasn't some bizarre tasing or torture device I had conjured up in the instantaneous horror movie scene I was playing in my mind, but rather it's an assistive device used by the visually impaired to get around, a white cane. The obsessively clean house with its military precision is not a sign of sociopathy, but rather a coping mechanism. All the puzzle pieces fall into place.

But... wait... not *all* the pieces fit. I replay all of our conversations over the past month and I can't remember a single instance where he referred to being blind. With all the intimate secrets we've shared with each other, you'd think this might have been one of them. This is not something I'd forget, even as emotionally banged up as I've been.

"Tayanita, you didn't leave me, did you?" he asks after I've been silent for several minutes. "You'd be surprised how often that happens to me. I can be having a whole conversation with an empty room and not know it."

"No, I'm still here. I'm gathering my thoughts," I answer tentatively. Corkscrew's purr is oppressively loud in the silence of the room.

"I'm sorry, Blue. I tried to figure out a way to tell you. I know you're probably disappointed. There is no real good way to work 'By the way, I used to be a helicopter pilot in the Coast Guard and now I can't see my hand in front of my face…' into the conversation."

"While I can see your point, I guess I don't understand why you thought it would matter to me. You know my most personal, horrific secrets — things about me that if other people knew, they would probably hate me. I trusted you. I laid my soul bare in front of you. Now, I feel stupid because you obviously didn't trust me to accept you as you are."

John makes his way over to me. He folds up his white cane and sets it on the side table. He holds his hand out toward me. When I extend my hand, he gently pulls me up to a standing position. He clutches my hand with both of his before whispering, "Do you mind if I touch you?"

I shake my head and then blush as I realize my mistake. "No, go ahead," I croak nervously.

I place my other hand on top of his and he slowly moves his hands up my arms and onto my shoulders. I'm glad I wore a long-sleeved cotton blouse and a light jacket for our hike tonight because inexplicably, the second he touches me, my skin breaks out in goosebumps and I have trouble catching my breath.

"I won't hurt you, Blue," he murmurs, as his thumbs graze my collarbones. "I'm still getting used to this. As a pilot, I'm a very visual person; or I was. My brain can't seem to get over the hurdle of translating what I feel into a picture. Maybe it's because I feel awkward practicing, but I've never quite gotten the knack."

"I can't imagine," I say. "Ketki tries to explain to me what it's like to have autism and sensory issues. She says it's like seeing too much all at once. I can't understand that either."

John's hands whisk over my hair. Because we had planned to go on a hike, tonight I braided it in a single rope down my back to keep it out of my way. I even took a little extra time with my makeup, which is not my usual habit. He follows my braid all the way down to the middle of my back. He smiles when he reaches the end.

"What?" I ask, self-consciously, unsure what to make of his smile.

John lifts his hand away from my head for a moment and rests his other on my shoulder as he says, "I may be blind, but I am still a guy. I love long hair. Does it go to your waist when it's unbound?"

I clear my throat nervously. "Not quite. I just got a haircut. It's a little below my shoulder blades."

"Do you mind taking it down so I can see?" he asks roughly.

I shrug. "After all the other stuff we've been through together, I guess we might as well reach a whole new level of weirdness."

"Like I said, conventional rules don't seem to apply to us," John quips.

I pull out the ponytail holder and place it around my wrist as I shake my hair out around my shoulders.

"You smell like green apples. I like it."

"Sorry, my hair is still wet. It takes forever to dry. That's my shampoo."

John weaves his fingers lightly through my hair and touches my scalp. The unexpected contact makes me jump.

"Oh, geez, I didn't mean to hurt you," John says as he removes his hands abruptly.

"You didn't. I'm nervous. I'm not quite sure how to handle this. Our relationship has thrown me for all kinds of loops. We're strangers on so many levels ... but on other levels, it feels like we are so much more. I don't know how to sort that out in my head and in my heart."

"I understand."

"No, I don't think you do, John. I told you things within minutes of meeting you over the telephone that took me years — I mean over a decade — to tell my own husband."

"Sometimes, things are meant to be."

"How do I trust that?" I stand still like a statue. "How do I trust us?"

"I don't know that I have any great answers. I can only tell you what my mobility coach told me when I first became blind."

I raise an eyebrow at him and wait for him to

respond, but then I realize my glances of subtle sarcasm are lost on him, so I ask, "He gave you relationship advice?"

John nods. "In a manner of speaking, I suppose he did."

"What did he say?"

"Whenever you're too scared to take a full stride, try to take half a stride because if you don't move forward, you make no progress."

I reach up and grab John's wrists and pull his hands closer until they are on my face. "That's probably the soundest relationship advice I've heard in a while. I'm willing to be brave if you are."

John runs the pads of his thumbs over my cheekbones and my eyelashes.

"Lady in Blue, why are you crying?" John asks with alarm in his voice.

I pull away from him and wipe my eyes with the back of my hand as I admit, "It seems as if you've discovered another chink in my armor. I'm not so buttoned up and put together. When I'm scared, I cry. The truth is I haven't been this scared in a while."

"Why are you scared? It's like you said, even though tonight is the first time we've officially met, we are far from strangers. I would like to think over the past month I have shown you I would just as soon walk into another copter blade than hurt you. You've had enough pain in your life."

"John, this isn't just about you, this is about me. I'm not sure I trust myself. Let's say, you're not the only one flying blind in this situation."

# Chapter Eight

# John

I'VE BEEN ON MULTIPLE victim rescues that were less nerve-racking than this conversation. If I ever thought I would come face-to-face with Tayanita, I would've probably handled things a little differently — but I was too busy having fun hiding under the cloak of anonymity. In the world of John and Lady in Blue, I didn't have to be blind. I could still be the capable person I once was. She didn't have to know how I struggle to leave my house and do everyday tasks like grocery shopping or how long it takes me to get the sports scores. I know it was a foolish masquerade. Yet, it was fun while it lasted. I felt accomplished and free in a way I haven't felt in a while. I could be the hero in all her escapades. I could be the answer to all her problems instead of a problem that needs to be accommodated.

"Oh Geez, I knew I shouldn't have said that. I'm so sorry. Sometimes, my brain kicks in about thirty-seconds after my mouth." Distress rings in Blue's voice.

"Tayanita, you didn't say a single thing wrong. I like your sense of humor, and I like that you're free with your words. I was thinking about our friendship and letting my mind wander."

"Wander where?" she asks. "It's not like we have years and years of friendship to look back on."

"I know, it's weird. It seems like we've been friends for a long time. Yet, it's only been a matter of weeks." I take Tayanita by the hand and feel my way to the couch. "Come on, let's sit down and make ourselves comfortable before we have this conversation. All this standing around is making me nervous. I feel like you will bolt at any second."

"I wouldn't do that. Contrary to my track record, I wouldn't leave without telling you."

"Good. Corkscrew isn't around to get squished, is he?"

After a few moments, she answers, "Nope, I don't see him. He lost interest in me quickly after my lap disappeared."

"He's learned to make himself scarce when I'm up and mobile. I've stepped on his tail a few times by accident."

I am relieved when Tayanita places her hand on my forearm to guide me down to the couch. I can do it myself, but having a steadying hand makes my descent a little less awkward. Depth perception is still an issue for me.

I hear her shift on the couch and I hear her shoes hit the floor. "You did say to make myself at home, right?"

"I did," I confirm.

"Here's something you should know about me, if you have something against bare feet, we probably can't be friends because I don't wear shoes unless I'm absolutely required to. In fact, it's probably the reason I still live in Florida."

"I like bare feet. I think they're sexy."

"You seem to think a lot of things are sexy."

"What can I say? I served in the Coast Guard — sometimes we had lots of hours to kill. Our conversations were not always deep and meaningful."

"You should hear what goes on during surgery. We've had more than one debate over the best fashions of the 90s or the best swear words of all time."

"So, you know what I mean."

"I want to know what you meant a minute ago; what were you thinking about when you were thinking about our friendship?"

I scrub my hands down my face as I try to find the words to explain my thoughts. "Blue, I don't want you to misunderstand this. I am so glad I can reach out and touch you. There were so many days I wondered if you were a figment of my overactive imagination, especially during the time I couldn't find your phone number. I wondered if maybe I dreamed up the whole encounter to distract myself from my tedious job. It seemed too good to be true. We've clicked like some Hollywood movie."

Tayanita laughs softly. "I thought I was the only one who thought that. I remember thinking to myself it was like a John Hughes romance."

"I didn't even want to tell anybody about our conversations because I was afraid I would somehow jinx them," I admit sheepishly.

"I felt exactly the same way! This is so weird." She squeezes my arm.

"But ... I had a whole other level of fantasy you didn't even know about. That's what makes this so hard.

As long as you knew me only as John and I knew you as Lady in Blue, you could envision me as a big strong hero and I could see you as the exotic woman in my mind that saves lives every day. But, now that you know who I am, you can see there is a reason the Veterans Administration doesn't believe I'm capable of doing anything other than selling random BS on the phone, and if there was ever an emergency, you would have to rescue me, not the other way around."

"John, you haven't been paying attention to what you've been doing in my life."

"I haven't been doing all that much; I've only been a sounding board."

"No, you've been so much more than that. You were there for me when no one else was. I was about to throw away what was left of my relationship with my daughter because I was consumed with guilt over my choices. The conversations you and I had gave me the room to breathe. They allowed me to step back and gain a little perspective on the person I was when I married Mark, when I had Ketki, and after I left. Do you know you are the first person to truly listen to me without passing judgment on my decisions?"

"How could I possibly judge you on your choices? I wasn't in your shoes. That would be like you trying to tell me what it's like to be blind."

"See? That's exactly what I mean. No one else in my life has your perspective. If you hadn't stepped up to be my friend, I would not have been able to have an honest and difficult conversation with Ketki the other day. I wasn't hiding anything from her at her birthday party. She could read every bit of stress on my face. Unfortunately, she misinterpreted it and decided it was because I hate her. I feel so bad; she doesn't deserve to think that. Nothing could be further from the truth. If anything, I hate myself for the choices I made."

"Blue, you don't deserve to hate yourself for what you had to do either." I squeeze her hand.

"You know the street works two ways, don't you?" she asks.

"What do you mean?"

"If I don't get to guilt trip myself for things I can't change, neither do you. I don't think you purposefully became blind or anything."

I sigh and run my hand through my hair. It is shaggy; I should probably get a haircut. I forget about these things since I no longer routinely catch my reflection in the mirror. It's one more reminder of all the things which have changed in my life.

"You're probably right, technically. The investigators from the Office of Marine Safety cleared me of any responsibility. They called it all a freak accident. It's true, in many ways it was. But I can't help but think of a dozen different decisions I could've made differently that would've saved a lot of people massive amounts of grief."

"Show me any emergency anywhere, and any professional worth their salt will give you the same breakdown. We can always do it better, safer and more proficiently especially if something went awry. I would imagine as a pilot, you and I share a lot of the same Type A personality traits. At least for me, that translates into finding a hundred different ways to blame myself if something doesn't go according to plan. Sound familiar?"

I nod tightly. "Very, but in this case, the shoe fits."

I jerk backward in surprise when Tayanita reaches her hand up and brushes my hair out of my eyes. "Will you tell me what happened?" she asks softly.

I tuck her against my chest as I lean back into the sofa cushions. "Are you sure you want me to tell you this? It's grisly. It's not appropriate first date material. This is not light and fluffy get to know you stuff."

"I wasn't aware I had given you the impression anything about my life was light and fluffy. I deal with grisly on a daily basis, remember?"

"Just because you deal with it on the job, doesn't mean you want to face it in your social life," I argue.

"John," she says in an exasperated tone, "let's go back in history a bit. If you'll remember, I told you I had thoughts of killing my daughter at one point. I'm sure whatever you have to tell me can't be worse than that."

"Worse? Maybe not. Different? Yes," I answer. "However you categorize it, it was catastrophic all the way around."

I can hear Tayanita unfold herself from the couch. "You want anything to drink? Water, pop, Jack Daniels?" she offers. "I have a feeling this might be a long conversation."

"I'll take a Coke."

"Straight?"

"Yeah, I think I'm better off staying clearheaded for this conversation."

"Okay, tell me which way to go for the kitchen." She trips over my foot.

"Do you need my cane?" I tease.

"Some days. It's probably for the best you can't see

my lack of grace, although it would provide some comic relief."

A familiar rumbling invades our space. For such a small puff of fur, his silly cat has the loudest purr I've ever heard come from a kitten. It's not because I've suddenly developed supersonic hearing either, even my family comments on it.

Tayanita laughs with delight. "Oh, look! Corkscrew is here to escort me to the kitchen. He must think he's going to get fed."

"In case he gets lost, the kitchen is straight back and to the left. If you're hungry, you can make some microwave popcorn. Corkscrew likes to play with it."

"That's all right, I'm just thirsty. I'll be right back with the drinks."

I listen as her feet softly hit the wood floor as she leaves the room. As I wait for her to come back, it occurs to me how much I miss pacing. I used to be an epic pacer. I can no longer do it comfortably I'm too aware of the world around me and the possibility of falling or running into something. My equilibrium is off now that I can no longer see. I miss the ability to work off excess energy as I process thoughts. The two were more closely intertwined than I ever thought they were. As I consider how to frame the conversation, my adrenaline edges up a few hundred notches. I don't think I've been this on edge since before the accident. I used to feel this hyper–aware of my mental processes and mental checklists before every mission.

I empathize with how nervous Tayanita felt before she made her disclosures. It's not easy to bare your tender underbelly to someone else and hope they don't judge you harshly for your mistakes. As I'm about to change my mind and decide that this whole weird experience is a colossal waste of time and destined to end in failure, I hear Tayanita's light laughter as she addresses Corkscrew.

"Come on. I'm tempted to call you Weeble-Wobble. I know you can make it. I saw you go chasing after that dragonfly. It wasn't the most graceful thing I ever saw, but you almost got him. I think maybe the unevenness of your attack makes you stealthier."

I think it's adorable that Blue talks to my cat. She strikes me as a logical, common sense kind of woman. It's a little disconcerting when she talks to my minuscule ball of fur as if he's another human being. It seems to soften some of her edges which can seem bristly when you speak with her.

Tayanita stands in front of me and taps me on my foot which is crossed over my knee as I try to sit here and act casual, as if I don't have another care in the world. The whole thing strikes me as a little ludicrous. We seem so domestic. You would never guess this is the first time we've ever met.

"Hope you don't mind, I put a few ice cubes in yours. I like my drinks nice and cold."

"I thought that was almost a prerequisite for living in Florida. Doesn't everyone use ice cubes as an internal air conditioner even in the dead of winter?" I ask.

She chuckles softly before answering, "Well, when you put it that way, I guess my tastes are not all that weird." Tayanita takes a deep breath and blows it out before coming to sit beside me like she was before. She rests her head near my shoulder before she continues, "Okay, enough stalling. We've got our usual drinks and comfy chairs, it's time for sharing circle."

I place my arm along the back of the couch and play with the ends of her hair.

"What color is your hair?" I ask abruptly.

Tayanita chokes back a laugh and clears her throat. "Stalling much? I bet your teachers loved you."

"I swear I will focus after you answer my question. This one thing has been distracting me for weeks, I need to know."

"I don't know, I guess it's nothing special. People can't even decide what color it is. Most people think it looks black, but other people argue it's more like a dark sable brown."

"Come on, I bet people compliment you on your hair all the time. You sound like my sister. My sister is beautiful, but she thinks she's a plain Jane."

"Oh look who's talking!" She lightly punches me in the arm. "You're not so bad looking yourself. You look like you could star in one of those military recruiting posters with your strong jaw and dimples."

"When I was new to flight school, I actually did. It was cringe-worthy — like, would you like some cheese with that burger? The photographer said it was because I fit the props. I think it had to do with a losing bet somewhere, but I never did figure out how I drew the short straw. I wasn't even the newest guy. I was razzed about that for a couple years." I run my hand through my long unkempt hair and wince as I admit, "It's funny, I'd like to trade places with the quasi-cool, completely naïve guy I was back then. Jaded, cynical, and diminished is not fun."

"I think it's time for you to tell me the story from

start to finish. I know it's hard. As they say — been there, done that. The good news is I did feel better when I was done. It's my turn to be here for you," Tayanita squeezes my hand. "Before you ask, my eyes are dark brown too. Some people say they look a little like obsidian."

"Sounds absolutely beautiful. Did I ever tell you I majored in geology? Rocks are kind of my thing."

"I thought things that flew in the air were kind of your thing —"

"Once upon a time they were," I answer as I lean forward and rest my elbows on my knees. I haven't told the story very often. Sure, I've told very abbreviated versions of it to doctors and counselors and the thirty-second version to coworkers, but I've never told the whole thing. This is painful on a soul level.

I carefully take a drink of the soda Tayanita brought me. After I set it down, I suck in a deep breath and continue with my story, "I never thought there would be a time in my life where they wouldn't be. I thought I'd be like Harrison Ford after I retired. I thought my wife, Josselyn and I would hop from island to island whenever we retired and she would go do her yoga while I watched the sunrise and took pictures of the wildlife. But … I got stupid."

"What do you mean?" I can almost envision the furrow in her brow as she concentrates on making sense of my words.

"It's hard to know where my litany of bad decisions started. I don't know if it was clear back when I watched Top Gun as a kid and decided I wanted to be that guy — the guy in charge. Or maybe it was in college when I decided to rely on coffee to work my way through school and the side job so I could have a fast car. Maybe it was falling for the girl who was clearly out of my league both in looks and an economic status. Then again, maybe we should've waited to get married. The ink was barely dry on the marriage license before everything in our world changed."

"I think that's standard of all couples who get married in their twenties."

"Possibly. Still, I think you'd find very few guys who were as totally gullible as me. I was sure we would beat all the odds. I was planning to be the conquering hero who would be saving the citizens of a grateful nation while my happy wife was holding down the home front."

"Again, not necessarily an insane expectation of a newlywed who is in love with his wife."

"The weird thing was that it all seemed to be going to plan. Josselyn seemed happy and my career was advancing as I expected. I loved being a Coastie, and I was a darn fine helicopter pilot. The only dark spot on the horizon was we were scheduled to go over to Afghanistan to help provide support for the peacekeepers."

"I wasn't aware the Coast Guard was involved in that kind of stuff. I thought you guys handled all the capsized cruise ships and fishing vessels and the people who decide to jump off the docks and cliffs. When I think of the Coast Guard, I think of drug interdiction and rescuing refugees who try to come by boat."

"We do all that stuff too, but we are an active branch of the military, even though we serve under Homeland Security. Everyone forgets we exist."

"I'm sorry, John, I didn't know. I didn't mean to be

disrespectful."

"It's all right, Blue. It's an old sore spot with me. The Navy fly boys get all the glory. A lot of our missions are as dangerous, if not more so."

"Obviously, the risks are great," Tayanita leans into my shoulder.

"They are substantial. But what was so unbelievably frustrating about 'the incident'," I say, using air quotes to emphasize my point, "is that it happened on a routine training mission as we were preparing our equipment to be mission ready. It simply shouldn't have been dangerous. Yet, it was."

"And you think you're somehow responsible?" Blue asks, disbelief clear in her voice.

"As a matter of law, no, but the rest of it's a little fuzzier."

"Why do you say that? You were cleared by all the authorities. Did you lie or something?"

"Oh heck no! I told them everything I knew and a few things my lawyer wishes I would have never said. I was more than truthful. Some of my former teammates are still not speaking to me."

"I hate that. You had a responsibility to tell the truth. You know, oaths and all that. I don't know why people expect us to be professionals one moment and then lie through our teeth the next," she says bitterly.

"Sounds like there's a story there," I tease lightly.

I can feel Tayanita shrug. "Someday I'll share it with you, but today you are holding the magic stone in the sharing circle. Today is the day for your story. So, why do you feel like you have more responsibility than other people?"

I heave a sigh as I realize this will make me look more like a zero than a hero in Blue's eyes. Still, I've come this far, honest is honest. To do that, I need to tell the whole story.

I take another swig of my drink before I launch into the most difficult section of my journey into literal darkness. "The part which wasn't adequately reflected in all the countless pages of reports was the role my attitude and ego played in the accident. By the time it all went down, I was known as the most levelheaded, experienced pilot in the unit. Not much flustered me. I'd become a little too comfortable in that role, I guess. Everything was a bit too routine. We had a new class of pilots and this one guy was clearly gunning for my job. He made no bones about the fact he thought the Coast Guard was second-class to the Navy and he was using our flight school as a leg up to get into the 'real' service. He had money and threw it around like it was confetti."

"What a charmer," Tayanita mutters. "I know a few doctors like that."

"As you can imagine, his attitude pushed about every button I had. My parents are completely awesome and love my sister and me to the moon and back. But my dad is a bus driver and my mom works as a city planner. Although they had tons of love to give us, if Katie and I hadn't gone to school on scholarship, it would have been tough going. We were taught you make friends, you don't buy them."

Blue replies indignantly, "Well, yeah!"

"It's safe to say this kid annoyed me. I could never tell if he was the real deal or if he was playing dress-up. One of the other team members thought he might be cheating on his coursework in flight school."

"Oh no, I can almost guess what's coming." Blue sucks in a breath.

"You may think you know, but it's like one of those complicated domino puzzles where everything has to fall into place for this catastrophe to have unfolded the way it did," I explain.

# Chapter Nine

# Tayanita

The fact that I can observe John while we're having this conversation without him knowing I'm watching his every move is both fascinating and almost a little distracting. At first, it was a shock for sure. I can't help but wonder why he never mentioned he's blind. I'm a medical professional, it's not like I'm going to think he has cooties or anything.

I'm trying not to treat him any differently because of his impairment, but it's those little things that keep tripping me up. I'm excruciatingly aware of everything I'm saying. Before tonight, I didn't realize how many idioms have the sense of sight at their root. I seem to be tossing out every bad pun on the planet. Some of them are intentional, but others seem to appear out of nowhere. I feel like my tongue is about twice its normal size every time I inadvertently blurt one.

John is struggling to tell me about his past. Since I am a surgical nurse now I don't get to hear as many personal stories as I once did when I was working my way up the ropes, but it's never easy for people to tell you about their biggest mistake, especially if they're honest about accepting personal responsibility.

Even with the few facts I have in front of me now, I can almost predict what he's going to tell me. I'm not sure if I feel worse for his damaged body or his broken heart. I wish this was like a book where I could simply skip the painful parts and get to the happily ever after. I don't want him to have to relive his pain. Yet, I know from personal experience sometimes there is no way around it.

The muscle in John's jaw twitches as he grinds his teeth and rubs his temples.

"Is this too much?" The nurse in me comes roaring to the surface.

He shakes his head. "No, I'm trying to figure out what to say."

"So, what happened with the wanna-be hotshot?" I prompt gently.

"The other senior crew members and I decided if he thought he was smarter than everyone else on deck, we'd give him a chance to show it. It didn't seem like he would listen to us anyway."

"I can't say I wouldn't do the same for a nurse whose bravado was bigger than their brains. Sometimes, they need to see what they don't know before they can figure out what they need to know."

"That was kinda what we figured would occur," John answers as he absently rubs the back of his head.

"I suppose that's not what happened?"

"I don't know for certain. I'm not sure anyone knows the exact sequence of what occurred next or its cause. The official finding was mechanical failure not otherwise specified. Whatever the actual cause, the upshot was I got smacked in the head by a rotor blade while I was double-checking his pre-flight inspection, and my world went dark."

"I promised I wouldn't wear my professional hat today, but it's a force of habit. Concussion is a no-brainer diagnosis. What do they say caused your blindness?" I ask, for a second forgetting John's living room is not a clinical setting. It's none of my business. I pause for a moment before I add, "You know what? You don't have to tell me. I'm not supposed to be in medical mode. I'm here as your friend."

John grins at my discomfort. "You do realize that my diagnosis is not the hard part of the story, right?"

I slump down in the couch a bit as I concede, "Right. I knew that. Sometimes I forget to take off my professional hat and the lines in my life get all blurry. If I get too pushy about all this, remind me that I'm not part of your medical team."

"It's not a problem. Sometimes I can use an outside perspective. Anyway, I mentioned that this story had many layers. A lot of them had to do with my own personal choices. In college, I tried to be everything to everybody. So, I became a huge coffee addict. I couldn't just make one bad personal choice, I had to make several. I added cigarettes to the coffee just for kicks. To keep my grades high enough to get into flight school and hold down a job, I was burning the candle at both ends. At that age you think you're invincible, and I was for several years. One bump on the head took all of my invincibility and crumple it like a used gum wrapper. No one knew I had an undiagnosed aneurysm. The concussion and resulting swelling was enough to make it rupture. The rupture caused damage to my optic nerves. It was a catastrophe waiting to happen."

"I take it you are not one of the lucky ones who got

your vision back after the swelling went away?"

"Not so far. The doctors tell me the more time goes by, the less likely it is that I will regain any vision. I guess there's a bit of a magic window and I'm outside of it at this point. I've tried to explain this to my family, but they don't want to accept the news."

"Traumatic injury is hard on everyone — victims and families alike. Your new reality post-injury is often nothing like you ever planned for your life."

"That's putting it mildly. I had planned on being a Coastie until I retired. It turns out the Coast Guard doesn't have much use for pilots who can't see."

"Yeah, I can see how that might be a problem. It would be a little scary to be rescued by a pilot who is blind," I say before I fully think about how insensitive my comment must sound. Sometimes my irreverent, sarcastic sense of humor impedes good old-fashioned common sense and manners. I cringe at my stupidity.

I let out a little hiccup of surprise at John's loud hoot of laughter.

"Are you okay?" I ask when I recover my breath.

"I'm good," John responds with a wide smile. "No, actually, I'm great. I can't tell you how refreshing it is that you say what you think like a regular person. I miss normal conversation. Everyone is so busy trying to protect me from words and ideas which might hurt me, no one just talks to me anymore."

"Okay … I guess I'm glad I could be a clumsy, insensitive oaf. You'll probably enjoy hanging around me because I specialize in being awkward and saying inappropriate things."

I start to re-braid my hair out of nervousness. I

bump his shoulder with my elbow as I reach my crown.

"What are you doing?" he asks with a puzzled expression.

I freeze in place with my hands still on the back of my head. "Umm, I'm messing with my hair. I do that when I don't know what else to do. I'm French braiding it to get it out of my face."

John chuckles. "After all the things we've been through together, this conversation is making you nervous?"

"Oh, I was nervous before, you couldn't see it because we were on the phone."

"Blue, I still can't see it." He tilts his head.

"Funny. I see what you did there. You're just trying to make me feel better."

He nods as he holds his hands up in front of himself in a placating manner. "I am. I plead guilty. I was a weirdly sarcastic, randomly inappropriate guy who you took in at your own peril before I got injured. I miss being that person. People are like flighty rabbits around me now. I am afraid if I show them who I really am, I might totally scare the crap out of them."

"Oh my Gosh! I feel the same way. I've got older brothers, but I was the first girl, so I was supposed to be different. I was supposed to be a good example for all the other kids, more nurturing, less bold and not so pushy. I think that's part of the reason Mark and I ended up married so young. We were both trying to escape the stereotypes our families had for us. We didn't realize we would lose ourselves in the process. It took me a long time after leaving Mark to rediscover the bossy, smart, sometimes completely nerdy woman I am. Sometimes, I think I'm still looking for her."

"I like you just fine. I love that we can shed our polite social masks around each other. I'll agree to ignore your nerdy outbursts if you'll look past my terrible jokes and awful puns."

"Okay, it's a deal but you may not know what you've gotten yourself into. Even my teenage daughter who is into all things computer, finds me unacceptably nerdy sometimes," I comment as I continue to braid my hair.

John must be able to sense my movements because he says, "Please stop. Do you mind wearing your hair down? I like the way it feels against my arm. It makes me feel connected to you. I miss that. It's like people are afraid to touch me now. I don't know if it's because they fear I might break or if they think blindness is somehow contagious but except for my mom and my sister, people rarely ever get close to me now."

I suck in a quick breath of air. What am I supposed to do with a request like that? His question plunges me right back into the weird space our relationship occupies. We are not a couple, yet in many ways, we are closer than anyone I've ever dated or been married to. Before I lose my nerve, I un-braid my hair and shake it out around my shoulders. I attempt to relax before I ask John, "What else do you miss?"

"You know, it's funny no one ever asks me about that either. It's like it's a taboo topic. It's not like I don't think about it. I'm confronted by the fact that I'm blind almost every second of every day. It's not like I'm going to say, 'Oh shoot, I forgot. Now that you reminded me, I am all bummed out.' Although, there is a moment almost every day where I completely forget. It's like reliving a bad breakup."

"I bet I know when that moment is," I whisper softly.

"Yeah? How do you know?"

"I know because I have the same moment every day. It's the moment between sleep and wake where the person you are in your dreams ceases to exist. In my dreams, I can be a perfect mom and wife and undo all the choices I made. In the space of a single breath, reality takes over and I am alone again to face the consequences."

John clears his throat as a look of devastation crosses his face. He's silent for what seems like forever. "I'm sorry, Blue. I was hoping you wouldn't understand. But, you're right. It's that moment when I forget who I am now as I get lost in the memories of who I once was. I hear the birds sing in the tree outside my house, and for some reason my brain has not yet acclimated to the fact that when I open my eyes I won't see the sun streaming in my window. I miss bird-watching at sunrise and taking hikes when the sun is barely coming up. I desperately miss taking pictures."

"I don't know what I would do if I wasn't able to be outside. Hiking is practically my religion. It is my refuge from my stressful job and the way I stay sane. It's great because when I'm out there, it doesn't feel so odd to be alone."

"Now, it's my turn to put my professional hat on — or shall we say my former professional hat? I'm sure you're aware it's a bad idea to go hiking by yourself. I can't tell you how many solo boaters I have helped rescue in my career. I miss that too. I miss being someone's hero. Somehow, selling herbal pet vitamins over the phone doesn't quite match up."

"We've already talked about this. You will always be my hero whether you want to accept it or not. Maybe we've been focusing on the wrong end of things. Are there any perks to being blind?"

John snickers. "Boy, you sure do like to ask the tough questions."

"Oh, it's not that challenging. I can already think of a perk. I don't even have to wear any makeup and you can imagine me to be as beautiful as you want me to be. It requires zero energy from me. Trust me, that's a big perk. After I've worked a double shift, I don't look so pretty. You won't ever have to deal with that mess. Bonus points for you! Okay, if I'm honest about it, there are bonus points for both of us - I'd rather skip the whole makeup routine myself."

John reaches out and brushes his fingers down the side of my cheek. "I'm taking a wild stab in the dark here, but I think I would probably find you beautiful under every circumstance, even if I had perfect vision."

"Wait a second. I need to duck from incoming puns," I quip.

"Hey now! You promised not to hold that against me," he protests. "I told you it would happen. I guess there's another perk. I can't tell if someone doesn't like what I'm wearing or if my joke doesn't hit the sweet spot. If they make a face at me, it flies right over my head."

"You don't have to watch bad reality TV. That perk should be worth gold."

"Wrong! I will only give you half credit on that. Have you ever tried listening to that stuff with your back turned? It's crazy. The only thing crazier is trying to sort out political pundits on the news without being able to see who is talking. They all talk over each other and soon they all sound the same. It drives me crazy."

"You're right. That would be enough to make me certifiably batty. I guess you've had to adapt everything you do. It must've seemed overwhelming."

"To tell the truth, sometimes it still is. But, some things have been good too."

"How so?" I ask, trying not to sound too skeptical.

"At first, I was sure I was going to hate everything about being blind. Don't get me wrong, it's still a struggle. Life is harder. But every once in a while, I'll notice I approach something differently than I did before and I'll realize the new way is better."

"Probably not when you're selling vinyl siding."

"Most often not," he answers with a smirk. "Still, finding you was a big perk. Usually, my enlightenment comes in smaller doses."

"Like?" I ask with all the patience of a curious toddler.

"Well, nothing like a big smack on the head to teach me I'm not all that. I rarely stride into a room like I own the place anymore. In retrospect, it's probably a good thing. I can't imagine how annoying that must've been."

"Hmm… I still think you're awesome, but these are your life lessons, so don't let me interrupt."

John shifts on the sofa and turns his face toward me. "I learned a big lesson about slowing down and stopping to hear what people say. Since I can't read all the nonverbal cues anymore I have to listen to what they're saying. I learned to hear what people don't say in the beats of silence between their thoughts."

John's words are straightforward enough, but something about their intensity in light of our intimate, personal conversations takes my breath away.

I lick my lips nervously before I ask, "Have you picked up anything special in our conversations?"

"More than you could possibly know, Tayanita. Never in my life have I been so grateful for that crappy job."

# Chapter Ten

# John

FOR THE FIRST TIME in I can't remember when, I am content to be awake. The transition between the old me and the new me went off without a hitch this morning. I suspect it has a lot to do with the fact that Tayanita is half-sprawled across my lap and soundly sleeping as if she doesn't have a care in the world. Even Corkscrew has joined the party. He's curled up in a tight ball in the crook of her shoulder purring like a boat motor. I don't blame him. I feel like purring this morning too.

This was not a planned thing. After Tayanita and I finished talking through my accident and how it impacted everyone involved, we decided there wasn't enough time to go hiking. So, we moved the picnic to my front room. Tayanita volunteered to prepare the sandwiches, so while she did that, I checked the scores on TV. That's when I was introduced to Tayanita, the football fan. Needless to say, she is not anything like I expected.

She was so jazzed I had taped the Bulls against the Golden Knights, she ran into the living room to give me a hug which almost knocked us both off the couch.

Finding a football fan in Florida is not hard to do;

we have four large schools which command a lot of media attention. This is the land of Tim Tebow, after all. However, I can almost never find anyone who loves the small schools as much as I do — or at least I couldn't before I met Blue.

Watching football used to be a great passion of mine. It was something I did with all my friends in a social setting and it was the perfect way to blow off steam. I used to watch it all from peewee games involving my friends' kids all the way through the Super Bowl. Radio coverage of football is okay, but it lacks the camaraderie and raucous good time of a tailgating party. Tayanita was amazing last night. Even when I could see, my friends never knew the names of the players of the teams I liked. She not only knew their names, but their stats and random trivia facts about them from various sports chat boards, websites and social media.

Tayanita wasn't sure how to help me at first. Truthfully, I wasn't sure how to ask for what I needed because no one had ever offered to be my eyes for something as trivial as watching my favorite sports teams. At first, she tried to sneak her color commentary in between the announcer's comments, but that quickly became frustrating. I have to hand it to her; she is brilliant. She came up with the solution of turning on the close captioning for the deaf so she could follow any news from the announcers, but she turned the volume off and provided the most amazing running play-by-play I've ever heard.

The woman knows her football. When the Bulls tried to pull a flea flicker, Blue was so excited I thought my eardrums would burst. It was exhilarating seeing it through her eyes. I also learned a lot. Every time there was an injury on the field, Tayanita would describe it in intricate detail and tell me the probable treatment and prognosis. After our third player went down with a probable torn meniscus, I told her she should probably withhold some of that information from me because I was falling into the depths of despair over the future of my team.

We had so much fun during the first game, she insisted on watching the other game I taped. It turns out she is a diehard fan of the Hurricanes. That commentary was even more colorful. She seemed to know everything there is to know about the team — right down to the number of kids the assistant to the assistant coach has.

When I commented about how exhausting it must've been for her to provide the running commentary for hours on end, she insisted she was fine and having a great time. The next thing I knew, she was curled up against my shoulder and sound asleep. I shut off the television and grabbed the throw blanket off the corner of the couch and covered us both.

It's been a couple of years since my divorce, and even longer since I've had someone sleep next to me. Josselyn was never a big cuddler. She was a night owl; and would often choose to watch television in the other room and stay there because my job required early morning wake-up calls. During the last couple years of our marriage, it had become a habit to sleep apart. I was naïve enough to believe all this was due to practical concerns. I didn't realize it was a symptom of my wife falling out of love with me.

On the days I am brutally honest with myself, I

know our divorce was inevitable, even without my accident. We matured in different directions. Instead of growing together, we grew apart. My blindness was the last straw for her. It was one change too many. It is fascinating Tayanita and I just met, but we've found a way to work together to overcome a small slice of my limitations. Josselyn never tried. Once it became clear that my sight would not be coming back, she gave up and decided it was more than she could handle. I never got a chance to prove otherwise. It still stings after all this time.

Tayanita shifts in her sleep and lets out a small sigh. Her hair falls over my arm and she snuggles closer. I weave my hand through her hair and rest it on her scalp. I love the feel of being anchored by her weight. Corkscrew is not so lucky and the change in position causes him to lose his balance and fall off his perch on Tayanita's shoulder. I'm trying not to laugh at his indignant yowl because I don't want to wake her up. She's been working for four days straight. Fortunately, she's got some time off so I am free to let her sleep.

As I have that thought, my phone rings. Tayanita sits up abruptly and winces when she encounters resistance from my hand. "Your thigh is vibrating."

"Sorry about that." I shrug and untangle my hand from her hair. "It's my mom. I'll call her later."

After a beat of silence, Tayanita says, "Maybe my job makes me paranoid, but it's early for your mom to be calling. I think you should probably call her back."

I roll my eyes at her. "I see how this goes; I don't even get to say good morning first." I stretch out my legs and reach down into my pocket to get my phone. "I guess I'll follow your advice and call my mommy, Nurse Moya.

She's probably calling to tell me the neighborhood cats are picking on the birds in her bird feeder again."

"Maybe so, but it's better to be safe than sorry. I'll give you a few moments of privacy. I should go feed Corkscrew anyway. He was trying to eat my earlobe earlier."

"Are you sure you don't like my cat better than me?" I ask as she walks away. She must be carrying Corkscrew because I hear him purring like mad.

"If you're hungry, I can get you some breakfast too," she offers. "Would you like eggs, cereal, or kitten chow?"

"You're quite funny considering how early it is. Let me call my mom and then we can decide how to handle breakfast."

I pull up the screen reader on my phone and hit my mom's number. I've gotten so used to the odd mechanical voice on my phone repeating every touch, swipe, and click I tend to tune it out most of the time.

"I always wondered how you dealt with stuff like that," Tayanita comments. The kitten, obviously tired of my interruptions, meows loudly. "Okay, Corkscrew thinks I have a date with his food bowl." I smile as I hear her footfalls across the wood floor.

When my mom picks up the phone, it is clear something is wrong. "Mom! Slow down, I don't understand what you're saying." I turn toward the kitchen and bellow, "Blue, come here please."

Tayanita runs back toward me and places her hand on my forearm. "What's going on?"

"I don't know!" I exclaim helplessly. "I'm trying to

figure that out." I shove my cell phone toward her. "Will you put this stupid thing on speakerphone and see if you can help me?"

She takes it from my hand and pushes the speakerphone button. We can hear my mom say, "Serving warrant ... officer involved incident ... under her vest ... critical condition."

Tayanita touches the back of my hand to focus my attention and asks, "Does your sister work in Gainesville?"

I shake my head. "No, she works for Alachua PD."

Before I can ask my mom any more questions, Tayanita addresses her. "Mrs. Ashford, they will take your daughter to Shands. They are the closest Level I trauma center. Try not to worry. I do know several of the doctors from the ED. They know their stuff."

"I'm not sure who you are, dear. But I'm glad you are there with Jonathan. We know we are going to Shands. Someone from the Gainesville Police Department is driving us there now. I called you from the car."

"I'll get there as soon as I can, Mom. Katie's tough. She wouldn't let something like this take her out."

"I wish the two of you would stop trying so hard to scare me to death. These dashes to the hospital are exhausting and hard on my nerves. I don't know why the two of you couldn't be accountants or something safer," my mom mutters. I am used to this conversation. It's one we've had many, many times before.

"It's because you taught us to be brave and strong and to serve others," I answer.

"Well, at this point I kinda wish I would've taught

you to chase the almighty dollar and work in a corporate office somewhere."

"Mom, we need to get on the road, so I'll see you later," I say.

"I love you, Jonathan." My mom sobs. "I love Katie too, but I forgot to tell her the last time I saw her."

"I know you do, Mom," I try to keep my voice even. "Katie does too. You'll get a chance to tell her soon."

After my mom hangs up, I look toward where I think Tayanita is standing. "Can I catch a ride to the hospital?"

Tayanita gently removes the phone from my hand and sticks it back in my pocket. "Sure. My only question for you is: do you want me to call in some connections at EMS so we can ride in the back of an ambulance? They might get us there faster if they treat it like a code."

"I appreciate the offer, but a regular mode of transportation will be fine. Alachua, is a ways away, and it'll take them a bit to get her here. I can't tell you how much I appreciate it though."

I can tell from the rustling sound she's probably braiding her hair again. "No problem. That's what friends do for each other, right?"

Her question brings me up short. Yes, I am very much Blue's friend. Yet, after last night, I'd like to take it up a few more notches.

I decide an artful dodge is in order. "Well, at least that's what we do today."

# Chapter Eleven

# Tayanita

I HAVE A NEW found appreciation for patients now. We have been waiting here for hours and no one has bothered to give us any helpful updates. Even Katie's captain hasn't been able to pry any information loose. This is my hospital, but my status and rank aren't giving me any special privileges. If anything, my coworkers are regarding my presence with a healthy amount of suspicion.

I guess I don't blame them. I've never mentioned having anyone important in my life, yet Mrs. Ashford is treating me like I'm her long-lost daughter-in-law. It's a little odd to say the least, but I guess we don't have time for awkwardness and the typical get-to-know-you routines.

"Nita, can't you call one of your friends and ask them what's taking so long?" Mrs. Ashford asks with a sigh.

"You have no idea how much I wish I could do that, but there are strict protocols on a trauma unit. Everyone has a job to do and if something interrupts the flow, it's not a good thing for the patient. I want the people on your daughter's care team to be completely focused on her."

Mr. Ashford coughs to clear his throat and cover his emotions like his son does. It is spooky.

"I suppose I understand. Even so, I don't think it's good news that it's taking so long, do you?"

"It's impossible for me to tell from out here. I don't know how many other cases they are juggling or if they might be waiting on the results of a medical test. There are too many variables."

"But you have some sense, right?" John presses.

He has dark circles under his eyes and I can read the stress in his face. He is trying to be stoic for his parents, but it's obvious that it is difficult for him to be here.

"I can tell you I have heard no alarming codes being called over the PA system and no acts like they are in full crisis mode. I think they're focused and they are doing what they do best. It's possible the person who is responsible for keeping us informed got called in on another case."

John lets out a deep breath. "Tayanita, please tell me you didn't say that to make me feel better."

I place my hand on his upper arm. "Of course I said it to make you feel better ... to make you all feel better, but that doesn't mean it's not true."

This is awkward. I haven't done this in a while. We are standing in front of John's door and I don't know what to do or say. So much has happened in the last twenty-four hours I feel like I'm watching someone else's life. I was completely accepted by a family who didn't know me from Adam. After they ordered John to go home and get some rest, they gave me a hug and said they look forward to seeing me at family dinners. It's been so long since I've had a sense of belonging anywhere I'm not sure what to make of the invitation. Now, I'm trying to decide what comes next.

"Why isn't Katie awake, Blue?" John asks me quietly.

"John, the bullet missed her vest by a fraction of an inch. It tore a good hole in her and it came close to some vital organs. The bullet nicked an artery near her heart and they had to cool her down to be able to do the surgery. Some people come out of that faster than others. But the protocol is solid and should help with her recovery."

"You're telling me Katie's still sleeping because she's cold?"

"And the fact that a .22 caliber bullet was bouncing around her thoracic cavity like it was a pinball machine. From what I understand, it grazed a couple of her ribs too."

"Is my sister going to die, Blue?"

"I don't get to decide that, John. Her vital signs are strong and she didn't take a direct hit to anything vital — only glancing blows. Only time will tell for sure, but based on what I know tonight, the odds are strongly in Katie's favor."

"Thank you for all you did today. You know, my mom totally loves you. They think you're the best thing since eggnog at Christmas."

"I thought they were great too. They were incredibly nice to me, given the fact I'm a complete stranger in your life."

"My parents are great like that. You helped your case a lot by being one of the smartest people I've ever met. It is clear my dad respects your opinion."

"I'm glad I could help. You need to get some rest. We were up late." I stand on my tiptoes to kiss his cheek. "I'm happy your sister is doing well. Good night, John."

As I turn to walk away, he reaches out and grabs the string of my jacket. "Wait! Where are you going? I don't want you to leave. I didn't mean to make it sound like I was pushing you out of here."

I stutter as I respond, "O - oh … um … You didn't. I figured you might want some personal space. It's been an intense few hours."

"You're right. It has been. If I ever needed a friend, it's now. I don't know what I would do if something happened to Katie. The two of us were inseparable."

"You *are* inseparable," I correct absently. "Katie's a little banged up, but she'll be fine. She's not gone yet; you can't start thinking that way."

"See, that's why I need you here. You know exactly how to save me from my spiraling thoughts. If you don't give me a kick in the pants and remind me what's good and true in the world, who is going to?"

"I guess I've been described in weirder ways."

"Please stay and I'll describe you however you want me to," John pleads as he rakes his hand through his hair.

"Okay, John you have to get some rest. Katie is going to need you," I say as I admit defeat and open his front door.

I am sitting in the middle of John's bed trying to answer all the emails and messages piled up in my in-box. I have been ignoring everyone's attempts to contact me over the last couple of days. The one from Ketki makes me smile. She was checking in to make sure my date didn't turn out to be a serial killer. She demanded visual proof I am fine. For once, I'm grateful John cannot see as he catches me in the middle of taking a silly selfie for Ketki. I quickly hit send and put my phone on the nightstand.

John is carrying a small tray of food. "Hey, I hope I'm not interrupting. I thought we could use something to eat. The candy bars from the vending machines didn't quite hit the spot for me."

"No, you're not interrupting. I'm sending Ketki an update to let her know I'm okay. I am starving, though," I say as I move to the edge of the bed. "I hope this isn't rude, but I'm curious how you're able to navigate with a tray in your hands."

John grins. "Of all the things I could do to impress you, this is it?"

"Oh, I'm impressed by a lot, but I'm curious about the mechanics of this," I retort.

"I'm busted. If you asked me to do this anywhere outside of this house, I'd be wearing our dinner. But, I've got the layout of this place internalized. Now, it's a matter of counting steps. About the only thing that trips me up is Corkscrew. If I trip over him, all bets are off."

"I think that's true of all of us whether or not we are sighted. My parents have a couple of dogs who believe their only mission in life is to trip you so you drop your plate of food."

"That's funny. Do you have any dogs?"

"Sadly, my work schedule is too crazy for me to have anything but a cat. Mr. Whiskers doesn't care if I'm around. In fact, sometimes I think he is annoyed when I'm home for more than a couple days in a row. He is a big fan of his automatic kibble machine. I think he would do fine in a world where I don't exist."

"It's funny how cats run the full spectrum of the affection-meter. I think you'll have to surgically dissect Cork from your arms when you leave. He seems comfortable there."

I lean forward to take the tray from John. It looks like a collection of fruit and cheese with a cup of some sort of soup. Without warning, my stomach growls loudly.

John raises an eyebrow at me as he asks, "Am I supposed to take that as a compliment or would you rather have something else to eat?"

"This looks like the most delicious thing I've had to eat in a while. I usually grab something from a fast food restaurant on the way home."

"Is this a case of 'do as I say, not as I do'?"

I smirk. "You betcha. If any of my patients ate half as badly as I do, I would pitch a fit. The sad part is I know better."

"Since the accident, I've been trying to eat cleaner.

My diet probably didn't help my risk factors any. Honestly, though, I still miss meat lovers' *pizza*."

"This looks good to me. If I had food like this around, the golden arches wouldn't see me quite so often."

"Well, I aim to make you comfortable."

I hold the tray still as John climbs into bed. I arrange the pillows behind our backs and grab an extra towel John had offered me for my shower and put it across our laps.

Without thinking, I guide John's hand over to the tray and show him where I placed the silverware.

"Drink?" he asks.

"Your drink is about at two o'clock on your right-hand side and your soup is at about nine o'clock on your left."

"Wow, I didn't even have to tell you how to do that. I'm impressed," John says as he places the paper towel across his lap.

I smile. "Once a CNA, always a CNA. Improving accessibility was part of my training. I guess I never forgot."

John picks up his spoon. "I guess all I have to say about that is, 'Thank God for small favors'."

I pick up my drink. "There's a lot to thank God about today. Your sister had a close call."

John picks up his can of soda and holds it up in the air as he says, "Here, here, I'll drink to that. To Katie's continued recovery and to us."

I gently click my can against his. "*Stiyineya.*"

"What does that mean?"

"Roughly translated from Cherokee, it means hold tight."

"That's what I'm doing. I'm holding tight to hope."

"I think we all are. It's all we can do."

I take a bite of soup and I'm pleasantly surprised to encounter a rich spicy flavor laden with curry.

"Usually when I have butternut squash soup, it's a little on the sweet side but I love this. Did you make this?"

"I wish I could take credit for it, but this one is all Katie. I'm still learning to navigate the kitchen well enough to cook anything beyond the basics. I don't want to burn anything down. My mobility trainer suggested I have someone with me for a while because it'll take me a bit to get acclimated. I haven't bothered to do much cooking-wise because I don't want to bother my family."

"That sucks. I don't cook because it's a pain to cook for one but I don't know how I would feel if I lost the ability. Maybe we can set up a cooking date soon."

"That would be great. I'd like to see us both comfortable in my kitchen …" John says, letting his speech trail off.

For a moment, the only sound in the room is our silverware against the dishes as I pause long enough to collect my thoughts. This is one of the reasons I haven't tripped all over myself to have relationships. I never know quite how honest to be. I've been known to be more than a little blunt and I don't want John to misunderstand what I'm saying because I'm not even sure what words will come out of my mouth.

John lays his spoon down as he says, "Did I say

something to upset you?"

I swallow hard before I answer, "No… I wouldn't say upset is exactly the right term. I think confused is the more appropriate term here."

"What do you mean?"

"You talk a lot about making me feel comfortable. First of all, you don't need to feel responsible for that. I can let you off the hook. I'm not afraid to stand up to people if it means defending something I care about, but for the most part I'm known for being awkward and shy. So, making me comfortable with everything might be a completely unattainable goal. I was born not quite fitting into my own skin."

"I don't want you to be at peace with the entire world, I want you to be comfortable with me and the kind of life I lead."

"See, that's where I get scared. I don't know where I stand with you or what makes the relationship between us what it is. I don't know what to do next. I've never been in this kind of situation before. I know I'm not the kind of person who could casually do the friends with benefits or Netflix and chill or whatever else they're calling it now. It's not in my make up to withhold my feelings like that."

A stunned look crosses John's face as he asks, "Are you under the impression I only invited you here tonight for a quick screw?"

"No … Yes … Maybe?" I waffle indecisively. "I don't know. I'm confused. I don't know if we're just friends or if we started dating without the actual dates."

John asks, "Are you done with dinner?"

Without thinking, I nod. After a few beats of silence, I recognize my error and say, "Yes, I'm finished. It was delicious. Thank you."

John moves the tray to the side as he shifts so I'm resting against his shoulder. "Tayanita, I don't have any great answers to all of your questions. I don't know what this is either. I know I'm happier when I'm talking to you than when I'm not and having you here makes me less restless — I don't know how else to put it."

"Okay —"

"But let me tell you what it's not," he interrupts. "I didn't invite you here because I need a quick roll in the hay. Shortly after I got my divorce papers from Josselyn, I did the whole meaningless, soulless, trashy sex thing. It felt good in the short run, but in the end, I felt like garbage. I knew better than to treat myself or anyone else like that. It didn't have anything to do with being blind. I was butt-hurt because my wife decided she didn't want me anymore. It took me longer than it should've to figure out the only person I was punishing was me. So, this is not that."

I cringe as I respond with far more candor than I need to, "I went through a stage like that too. It wasn't too many years after Mark established Hunter's Crossing. He and his buddies from law school started a law firm. For whatever reason, they picked up some rich socialite for a client and the media had a field day. Mark is an imposing guy and every time he would scowl at the cameras, it would make the news. The client was hanging all over him and dropping innuendos about the nature of their relationship. Even though my head knew better, my heart was convinced he had fallen in love with her and moved on to a life with the rich and famous."

"Did you ever get Mark's side of the story?"

"No ... I told you — I'm a big nerd with lots of book smarts, but I have the social skills of a hamster who has undergone a lobotomy. Rather than face down my fears directly, I decided everything I was seeing in front of me was true. I started lashing out at myself for my decision to leave Mark. Of course, at the time I didn't have the perspective to see that. I was simply too angry. I thought I was being edgy and moving on. I never even bothered to confront Mark."

"It sounds like you might still be in love with Mark," John suggests.

I shrug. "I won't lie. There will always be a part of me that loves Mark. He is the father of my child — our split didn't change that. Much to my surprise, the fact I was absent from her life for almost eight years apparently didn't either. But, he has Shelby now."

"That has to hurt a lot," John kisses the top of my head. "I'm sorry."

"If I had actually been more in love with Mark and less in love with the hope of how I thought things would go once I was married, I think it would be harder. Besides, it's almost impossible not to fall head over heels in love with Shelby. She's exactly what Mark needed in his life."

"You are being way more understanding than I think I could be. Maybe it's because Josselyn and I left so much unsaid in our relationship. I heard a rumor she's found someone and they are going to get married soon. Even so, I have no desire to come face-to-face with either one of them. That makes me sound like a huge jerk, doesn't it?" John asks.

"No, I don't think so. I think it makes you sound real. You forget — I've had many more years to get my emotional crap together. Still, I'm not all that together. The night you called me, I was in the middle of a breakdown of epic proportions. You probably didn't expect all that when you called to sell me siding, did you?"

"You're right. I wasn't expecting to find someone who gets me on so many levels. I wasn't looking to find someone to stand with me and my family on one of the scariest days of my life. For all the reasons I absolutely hate my job, I am forever grateful for it because I found you. It doesn't matter to me what we call this between us — or even if we give it a name. I can't help but believe I am meant to be in your life and you're meant to be in mine."

"When you put it like that, how can I possibly argue? I am not a big believer in coincidence." I lean over and kiss him.

He groans and kisses me harder.

"Please tell me this is real and not a coincidence," he says as he pulls away and catches his breath.

"As far as I'm concerned, this is as real as it gets," I snuggle closer.

"Oh thank you! I was beginning to wonder if all this was a great dream," he says in a hoarse, broken whisper.

# CHAPTER TWELVE

# JOHN

TWENTY-TWO STEPS EAST and west; five and a half steps
north and south.

That's how much space is at the end of Katie's bed.
I've been here often enough I can now confidently pace
without the use of my cane. It feels like I've been walking
for miles. But I don't know what else to do. I hate the fact
that I am no longer a rescuer. I can tell the difference in
the tone of voice in the medical staff. As a pilot, I was
once considered part of the team. I know EMS personnel
and life flight nurses across five states and in countries
I'm not at liberty to talk about. Though the staff has said
nothing to me directly, there is an underlying note of pity
and a distance that wasn't there prior to my injury. It is
enough to drive me absolutely insane. I feel like I'm the
kid on the playground who hasn't been invited to play
dodgeball and has to watch from the sidelines.

"Are you done stewing over there, or do I need to
order you some beer and peanuts to go along with your
mood?"

"You're barely off the ventilator, are you sure you're
ready to give me sass?" I tease.

"I am your little sister, it's my job." I hear her take a strangled breath and moan.

"You gotta help me out here, I don't know what happened." I try to keep the panic out of my voice.

"Relax, Johnny," she says unevenly. "I moved. It turns out getting shot hurts. It's not like in the cartoons. I feel like my whole Saturday morning existence while we were growing up was all one big lie."

"If it's any consolation, I heard your coworkers talking. The bad guy can't hurt anybody else. He's dead."

"That's what I understand. But what they don't know until they get final ballistics back is whether it was my gun which took him out."

"Shouldn't they have those back already? It's been several days."

"I guess you're right. I forgot how many days I was completely out of it."

"I can't forget about them, you scared the crap out of me. You are not allowed to do that again. I think I've aged thirty or forty years."

"That's about how I felt when you got hurt too. So, I suppose we're about even."

"You know Mom and Dad will put us in the room with nothing but down pillows soon, don't you?"

Katie groans. "I don't know how I feel about that. Right about now, that seems like a great game plan. I wonder, how long will I feel like crap?"

"I'm sorry to be the bearer of bad news, but Tayanita says it'll be three or four months before your ribs feel a hundred percent," I answer without thinking.

"Who's Tayanita? I don't remember that name. Right

now, I'm a little fuzzy. Is that the specialist who's coming into check out my heart injury?"

Her question makes me stop and think about how much has changed since the family dinner we had a few weeks ago.

"Umm … She's a friend," I answer vaguely.

"Oh my Gosh! You did the pause. You so totally paused before the word friend. You better spill. I've been laying in this bed for days and days and days with nothing to look at except for bad TV so I need some news — like right now."

"Geez Katie, I haven't gotten engaged yet or anything."

"If you don't tell me, I will just ask Mom and you know what kind of conversations that could lead to," my sister threatens.

"Wow, you took it up a notch. Things just got serious," I answer with a chuckle. "I'll answer your questions, Officer Ashford. There is no need to threaten cruel and unusual punishment."

My sister starts to laugh but then lets out a sharp yelp of pain. "I keep forgetting I can't do that. Stop making me laugh. Tell me what's going on. I notice you're looking a little less scraggly these days. I figure there must be a reason behind it."

"Tayanita did that too," I disclose. "It turns out she's got lots of siblings and is handy with a set of clippers."

"Where did you meet her? What does she do? Do I need to do a background check on her?"

"Katie, stand down. I met her because I called her as part of my job. We instantly clicked and met outside of my work."

"Oh Man! Johnny, do I have to give you the same lecture I give teenagers about safe dating in the digital age?"

"No, you do not have to school me on Internet safety. I'm good, thank you. Tayanita is actually a surgical nurse here at this hospital."

"Did she work on my case, because that would be weird? If she met the insides of me before she met the outside of me, I'm not sure I would know what to talk about with her."

"She was not working on the day we got the call. We were at my house."

"Wow! That's huge. I was shot before the sun came up. You never have people over. Did I interrupt something fun?"

"I think you're a little sister who knows entirely too much about my social life," I tease.

"Do I lie?" she asks pointedly.

I unfold my cane and use it to navigate over to the recliner chair next to Katie's bed. After I sit down, I answer, "No, your assessment is scarily accurate. I wish I could give you an easy answer about what's going on between Blue and me. But there isn't one."

"You are so busted! You used to rag on me all the time for using nicknames with my boyfriends, yet it seems the mysterious Tayanita has one."

"There's a story behind that. We talked for about a month before I actually knew her name. So, I used to call her my Lady in Blue."

"Oh good Lord! Do I need to run her through vice?"

I choke back a snort of laughter. "No, you do not. There were extenuating circumstances, which I am not at liberty to explain. She is a very solid, professional nurse with a lovely teenage daughter."

"You are frighteningly gullible. I thought you were the big brother. She's probably looking for a sugar daddy or something."

"Katie! That's enough. She wasn't looking for anything. I called her, remember? I was selling the woman vinyl siding. Do you think she was sitting by the phone waiting for me to call?"

"I don't know. It sounds bogus to me," Katie answers stubbornly.

"It was an unexpected twist of fate, but there was nothing nefarious about it. Tayanita is one of the most exceptional women I have ever met in my life."

"Still —" Katie interjects.

"Katie, please stop stressing out about this. I don't even know if there's something for you to worry about. I like Tayanita. I like her a lot. For now, she is my friend. Only my friend."

"John, I'm not buying it. There's something about you that's different. I haven't seen you this way since I can't remember when. It's almost as if you have found your hope again. There has to be more to it than that."

"She likes college football and roots for the 'Canes," I explain helplessly. "The rest of it is not my story to tell, but I need you to give her a chance. Please?"

"Okay, it's not like I'll be up to playing police officer anytime soon anyway. I'll try to be nice. But, if something seems weird to me, will you listen?"

"I always listen to you," I answer. "Speaking of relationships, I haven't seen your latest beau around. Shouldn't he be here?"

Katie sighs. "Turns out Vinnie the Pooh isn't so supportive of me having a career in law enforcement after all. It seems he has issues over perps shooting at me."

"That's too darn bad. Tell him to find a brain and a backbone and get his butt here," I growl.

"I decided if he wasn't willing to fight for me and my career, I wouldn't bother fighting for him."

"How did you get so smart?" I ask as I reach out for Katie's hand.

She grabs it and squeezes lightly. "I had a brave big brother who taught me all the important lessons in life."

The barista at the coffee shop was more than happy to help me locate Tayanita once she saw the flowers in my hands. Right now, I'm standing in front of her waiting for her to notice my presence. I'm guessing from the sudden absence of noise around me, other people have noticed and are waiting to see what happens. I know she's reading an intense crime novel. She was telling me about it last night and I can hear her turn the pages and the faint sound of music coming from her headphones. It could be a while before she notices me. When Blue disappears into her reading zone, it takes her a long time to surface in the real world.

I clear my throat and hear her gasp. "John? What are you doing here? Aren't you supposed to be at work? Is Katie okay?"

I hand her the bouquet of flowers as I say, "Katie's fine. The job is a long story. I came to eat lunch with one of my favorite people on the planet."

"Thank you, the flowers are beautiful. Sit down. I just got here and ordered my Panini, you should be able to order too."

"Excuse me, Sabrina can you take John's order?" she says to someone as they place drinks on our table.

The side of a cold water glass touches my hand. I can tell from her perfume it's the same person who helped me earlier. When the barista sees it's me, she asks, "You want your usual?"

"That'd be great, thanks." I stretch my shoulders and take a sip of my water. After the barista walks away, I ask Tayanita, "Is it me, or is this day dragging on like it's going to last a hundred years?"

"Our first surgery was at 06:30 this morning, so for me the answer is yes. I'm curious what's going on with you. If you ask a question like that, you have to know I'm going to ask about the job first."

"Let's just say McFerran and I couldn't come to an understanding about what was required for me to take vacation time to see Katie. Apparently having a sibling in the hospital recovering from a gunshot wound is not enough of a reason to miss my shift — at least not in his world."

Tayanita whistles between her teeth. "I think I know you well enough by now to know you told him to take his job and shove it."

"Well, there might've been a few more cuss words involved, but that was the gist of it."

"I'm sure I'm supposed to say I'm sorry you lost your

job. I can't bring myself to do that since you hated it with every fiber of your being."

"That's kind of how I feel about it too. But my reasoning might be a harder sell to the VA."

"I can't even begin to tell you how much I hate that for you. You should not have to justify quitting a job where the boss treats you like dirt."

"I know. But, that's a worry for a different day. By the way, I may have spilled the beans about us to my sister."

"May?" Tayanita presses.

"Okay, so I did," I concede. "I don't know if it's the little sister thing or what. She can always get me to say things I never intend to."

"Let me guess … she's not my biggest fan —"

"No, I thought that was weird. I expected her to be happy I'm out being social again, but instead she's grilling me like a suspect."

"John, you have to look at it from her perspective. I look sketchy as heck. You met me making a cold call. I'm a single mom, even though I don't have custody of Ketki and that in itself is going to open up a whole other can of worms. To top it all off, she knows I'm already spending the night at your house. I wouldn't be surprised if she isn't on the phone with her colleagues right now asking them to run my priors."

"If the two of you can ever sort out your differences, the world is going to be a scary place for me. That's almost a verbatim list of all her concerns. I don't know how you did it."

"It's easy. I'm a sister. If it was one of my siblings, I would feel the same way."

"Then we'll have to work on changing her perspective. I don't plan on eliminating you from my social circle anytime soon."

# Chapter Thirteen

# Tayanita

I'M NOT EVEN SURE why I'm here. This is about forty-five thousand kinds of awkward. Yet, here I am in Mark's law firm, being escorted to his proverbial corner office. My ex-husband has come up in the world since the days when he used to spread legal briefs out on the front room couch to sort them. In countless little ways, his law firm reflects his quiet, powerful leadership style. It isn't in-your-face opulent, but everything here spells confidence and success.

The receptionist escorts me back to his office and offers me a seat. "Mr. Littleson will be with you shortly, his conference call is wrapping up."

I can almost hear my heart pound as I wait for Mark to appear. I notice a beautiful picture of Ketki and Shelby collecting stones and feathers from the beach sitting on Mark's desk. I am a little surprised when I don't feel the familiar stab of pain in my heart when I examine a half a dozen family photos of them together. Happy looks good on him.

"Nita, what brings you by? Is everything all right with Ketki?" he asks with concern as he walks into his office with a stack of files in his arms.

"She's great. We are going to go see a movie this weekend." I show him the picture I'm holding. "Why haven't you and Shelby gotten married?" I blurt.

Mark sets down the files and studies me as if he's trying to evaluate how much to reveal to me. Finally, he sits down in his big leather chair and says, "I don't know. At this point, I'm not sure. First, it was her battle against cancer and then it was Savannah's ongoing legal problems. Now, it's a big mystery. Maybe she's suspicious of the fact you and I are friends? Perhaps she is waiting for you to find happiness first. I'm quite frankly out of theories. I would have married her years ago, if it was my choice."

"Is everything okay with her health?. Have you been fighting?"

"I probably shouldn't be talking about this with you — a marriage counselor might have a field day with this. But, you were my friend a long time before you were my ex-wife."

"True. I can't remember a time when we weren't. Even when I wanted to hate you, I couldn't bring myself to."

"In answer to your question, health-wise, things seem to have stabilized with Shelby. You can see from the picture she seems amazingly happy and Ketki is completely in love with her. We haven't been fighting. The only issue that's ever been between us is my relationship with you."

"I didn't know there was an issue. We sorted that out years ago. I told her I had my chance with you and I completely blew it. I thought she understood you and I work much better together as exes than we ever did as husband and wife."

"I know, I thought you guys had figured it out too. However, I think it's hard for her to see you all alone floating around on the edges of our relationship," Mark comments.

I blush. "It's funny you should mention that. I am not so alone these days. That's why I'm here. I want to help my friend and I need your assistance. I can pay you for your time, of course."

"Nita, if there's something I can help you with that's standing between you and happiness, I'd never charge you. Don't be ridiculous."

"Thanks, I appreciate that. But, before I tell you the whole story, you have to promise not to jump to any conclusions. Fate is a very funny thing."

"I don't know if I like the direction this conversation is taking. You're scaring me. You know I don't believe in coincidences."

"I don't either which is why it's completely bizarre that a random phone call from a guy named John may have saved me from myself."

*Etsi,* why do you look so sad? Shelby says this is a party. Ink'd Deep is like my favorite place in the world. I thought you liked it too," Ketki asks as she picks through a plate of appetizers.

"I'm fine. I'm just tired. It's been a long week. I wasn't expecting to go anywhere tonight. I'm so exhausted I might fall asleep."

Ketki pulls up her sleeve and shows me a glittery tattoo. "I don't think that's a good idea. Marcus is giving people temporary tattoos. He might give you something weird if you fall asleep."

I yawn. "I'll keep that in mind. I bet you were excited. You've been thinking about designing your own tattoo for a while."

"I know, but Marcus is silly. He put a smiley face and a big nose on my feather. He should know I'm too old for that kind of stuff now."

"I think it's cute. I like the shiny party hat. Do you know why we're having a party on a Tuesday night?"

"I don't know. I don't think anyone knows. It's a big mystery. Even Marcus doesn't know — and he owns the shop."

"Hey, Mark, do you know what's up?" I yell over to a table across the room where Shelby and Mark are playing poker with Isaac and Rosa.

Mark shrugs. "Not a clue. It was all very cloak and dagger. We were only told to show up and bring as many people as we could."

"I was wondering because I've worked two singles and a double shift in a row and I'm dead on my feet. I don't want to miss something important though."

"Well, it's a good thing for you Declan and I are here and the party can begin," Jade announces grandly as she strides over to the Bell of Prosperity.

"Oh, let me do it," Ketki offers as she springs to her feet and jogs over to where Jade and Declan are standing.

Declan bows in her direction as he hands her the cord to the old-fashioned fire bell. "By all means, we would be honored. Do you remember how this goes?"

Ketki's brow furrows. "I think so."

"Then, feel free to start whenever." Jade instructs.

Ketki turns to Shelby. "Mom, will you get me the step stool Rogue keeps in the broom closet?"

Mark gets up and goes toward the break room. "It's okay, I've got it."

I watch that interaction with a weird sense of detachment. It's clear they do this several times a day and think nothing of it. But, instead of feeling left out of the circle this time, I'm grateful we're all part of the same circle.

Mark brings back the step stool and picks Ketki up and sets her down on it.

"Dad!" she protests, as she squirms out of his grasp. "Knock it off! I'm not a little kid anymore."

Jett laughs out loud. "Sorry kiddo, your dad is going to feel the same way about you when you're thirty-five. I think you're out of luck."

"Oh, great. I was hoping he would outgrow that," she mutters to herself. Ketki clears her throat loudly as she asks, "Can everybody hear me? Okay, I guess that was stupid. There are not a lot of you here. So, I'll just go ahead."

I think about taking a picture to show John, but it only takes me a moment to realize it would be pointless. Still, I want to remember today. For whatever reason, today is the first time it has occurred to me I've figured out a way to be happy and find a place where I can breathe. It took me long enough, but it's a nice place to be. I snap a picture as Ketki gets ready to address us.

Rectify

"Welcome to Ink'd Deep. This is a special place; a place where my soon-to-be stepmom met my dad and a place where we celebrate good news. From the silly smile on Jade's face, I think she probably has some news to share with us. So, what do we do here at Ink'd?"

"We ring the bell!" We all answer in unison as we start to stamp our feet. I am a relative newcomer to this tradition, but apparently, it's been going on for years at Ink'd Deep. If someone has good news, everyone in the shop stops what they are doing to celebrate with the client. It's a simple but powerful tradition that celebrates gratitude.

Ketki pulls on the rope to move the clapper as we all cheer.

When she's done, she hops back up on the step stool. "I'm supposed to announce the good news now. But I'm clueless, so I guess my part is done. Jade, it's your turn." She runs back to our table.

Jade turns to Declan. "Do you want to tell them or do you want me to?"

"Normally, I would hog all the attention but I'll let you have a turn for a change," he jokes as he winks at us.

She kisses him soundly before turning to us and announcing, "You guys have no idea how hard this was to keep a secret. But... Look!" she says as she holds up her hand and displays a shiny new wedding ring.

Her parents look like they are in complete shock.

Diamond recovers first and asks, "When did this happen and why weren't we invited?"

"You are my only daughter," Jett protests, "I don't understand."

"Don't worry about it Daddy, we'll still have a big celebration soon, I promise. You'll still be able to do all the 'Dad' things."

Rogue walks up and hugs her boss as she says softly, "You better hurry up and tell the rest of the story, or people will jump to some interesting conclusions."

Declan nods. "Good point, Rogue. It was a spur-of-the-moment decision. Jade came with me on this trip because Aidan O'Brien needed me to help out with a concert in Vegas. Jade and I have been trying to figure out how to juggle her school schedule and my recording duties with Aidan. Finally, it seemed like the easiest thing to do would be to get the marriage part out of the way and throw a big party later after we get our schedules straightened out."

Jett practically growls at Declan. "Are you saying marrying my daughter was something you checked off your to-do list like picking up the dry cleaning?"

"No, sir. I would never dishonor her that way. Jade is as important to me as the music in my soul," Declan answers solemnly.

"Daddy, I know we're not doing a very good job explaining it, but it's not like that, really."

"What do you mean, honey?" Diamond asks.

"Mom, my husband is being really great. He's protecting me. Honestly, planning the wedding was driving me crazy. I was trying to please everybody and jam myself into a cookie-cutter mold of what a bride should be like. You know me well enough to know that never works for me."

I grin at Jade's description of wedding planning. I remember feeling much the same. It was like I was losing myself in the process of making everyone else happy. Somehow, I can't see Jade doing anything in the usual manner.

"Anyway, I got to the point where it was crazy. I started thinking if I could only pull off an amazing wedding, my whole life would be perfect. I lost track of how much I love Declan. It isn't the ceremony which counts, it is the fact we'll be there for each other. So, we solved the dilemma while we were in Vegas. Now we're married which was the point all along."

"Congratulations, I think this is a great thing," adds Ivy, Rogue's twin sister. "It means Rogue and I won't have to go shopping for a bridesmaids' dresses. I count that as a universal win."

Jade laughs out loud. "See, Daddy? It's not all bad."

"I don't know. I'm not convinced; I had plans to walk you up the aisle," Jett maintains.

"You'll still get to. We're going to do it later."

"When is later?" Jett presses.

"Well, we thought at my record release party would be a great time to renew our vows so you guys can all be part of it."

"I'm holding you to that, son. My girl deserves more than a drive-through wedding."

Jett's attitude makes me smile. My dad would sound the same way. Even at my age, I think he would have issues with me if I pulled a stunt like that.

Ketki's hand shoots up in the air. Jade smiles at her. "Ki, you know this is Ink'd Deep, right? You don't have to raise your hand like it's a classroom."

"Oh, I know. I wanted to let you know I have a

question," she explains.

"Shoot," Declan says, "we figured there would be a bunch."

"Well, I actually have two questions. Did you get married by an Elvis impersonator, and does this mean my dad and Shelby are next in line? I've been waiting forever for them to get married."

Jade chuckles. "No, sadly there were no Elvis sightings, although, that would have been epic. A very nice woman named Stargazer Eloise Rainbow had the honors."

"Not that I'm a skeptic or anything," Mark comments. "But you might want to check that one out and make sure everything's legal."

"Trust me, we did. She showed us a whole folder of documentation. Apparently, it's a request she gets quite frequently. I even double checked it with the DMV."

"What about Shelby and my dad?" Ketki persists.

"Ketki, that's not something Jade can answer for you; it's between Shelby and your dad," I say.

"I'm kinda with Declan on this one," Mark admits. "If I'd had my way, Shelby and I would've been married a long time ago."

Shelby drapes her arm around Mark's shoulder. "Jade's shoes feel very familiar to me too. I'm trying to make sure everyone is happy and no one gets hurt."

I look directly at Shelby. "In case I haven't been clear enough. I'm good with you being Ketki's stepmom. Just because Mark and I couldn't make it work together doesn't mean I don't want him to be happy."

Shelby springs up from her chair and comes over to

give me a hug. "Do you mean that? Mark is my happy. But you had him first; I could never make those things make sense. My definition of happy should not have to mean you are unhappy."

"Shelby, it's never been like that. I swear. Besides, these days I'm working on my own definition of happy."

Ketki looks over at Jade. "I don't know what just happened, but I think it's good. But, this has to be one of the weirdest parties I've ever been to."

Although I say nothing out loud, I can't say my daughter is wrong.

# Chapter Fourteen

## John

I MOVE GINGERLY AS I try to find the ice packs in my freezer. I am cussing like the military man I once was. I don't know why my mom thought it would be helpful to rearrange my entire freezer, but I can tell you it's not helping me find my ice packs. Finally, I give up and grab a container of frozen juice concentrate. Cold is cold at this point.

I am so frustrated by this whole day I miss the sound of Tayanita's key in the front door.

"Oh my Gosh! What happened to you? That looks painful," she exclaims. I can hear the sound of her feet as she scrambles over to me.

"It is painful, but luckily for me I can't see it. I guess that's one of those perks we were talking about."

She lifts up my shirt to look at my torso. "Okay, but what about my other question? What happened to you? You were fine this morning when I left for work."

I hold the container of juice close to my ribs and wince. "I wish it was that simple. I managed to get myself hit by a car."

"What?" she exclaims in a horrified voice. "I thought

you tripped over Corkscrew or something."

"No, I got clipped by somebody's side mirror today." I admit with a grimace. "I went to the employment office to see if I could get some help to search for a new job. That was a nightmare in and of itself, but then I went to go get coffee. I was in the crosswalk and the light told me to go, so I went. Apparently, somebody was in a hurry to get back to the office after lunch and they turned against their light. We had an unfortunate meeting in the middle of the crosswalk and I lost."

"Are you okay? I can't believe you were hit by a car. I have so many questions." Tayanita gently removes the juice can from my hands. "First though, I need to find you something better to use — you are not getting much contact with your wound this way. Do I need to take you to the hospital?"

"I hope you have better luck finding them than I did. My mom rearranged everything and now I can't tell where anything is. I couldn't find a stupid ice pack, so this had to do."

Tayanita's voice grows further away and I hear her rummaging in my freezer. "Oh, here they are," she says before she slams the freezer door. "Should I call your parents? They'd probably want to know."

"No, you don't need to call them. They don't need to worry about one more thing. Katie just came home from the hospital. I don't think I need to go hang out there. It's not that bad. I'm a little banged up," I insist as I try not to break out in a cold sweat. "I'll be fine after some rest."

"I appreciate your considered medical opinion, 'Dr. Ashford', but why don't you let me take a look. Sometimes, my nursing background comes in handy," she argues as she places her very cold hands on my rib cage and I jump. As she starts to gently probe around using her fingers, it's all I can do not to start a new round of cussing.

"You're very stoic. If I were you, I'd be bawling like a baby or passed out on the floor," Tayanita says after a couple of moments "That injury looks grisly. It's swollen and bruised already. How fast was this person going when they hit you? Did anyone witness the accident? What happened to the creep who did this to you?"

"I have no way of knowing if anyone actually saw it happen. I couldn't have been hit too hard. I didn't hear him coming, but I was able to get up afterwards." I shrug. "It didn't seem like anyone knew who the driver is. The jerk took off right after the accident. I wasn't even off the ground before they split."

"Where did you say you were when this happened? I bet the accident was captured on someone's surveillance camera."

"I went to an employment workshop and there was this coffee shop on the way that smelled delicious even from the sidewalk. I decided when I finished with my class I would go there and grab a cup. Unfortunately, I didn't even get to make it in the front door."

"Do you remember what this place was called? Maybe I can call them and see if anybody reported seeing anything."

I raise an eyebrow at her. "Well, the signs were hard for me to read from my vantage point."

"Right. I don't know why that keeps slipping my mind," she answers with an embarrassed laugh. "It's too bad you don't know where you were. I'd like to nail this idiot on a traffic-cam or something. This jerk should not get off scot-free. I mean, everyone knows not to turn into crosswalks. You should be able to go get coffee without being run over by a car."

"I don't know, it was all chaotic and one big blur. It could be because I was a little loopy and trying to get my wind back, but people kept trying to tell me to have a tough break. It was confusing."

"Hanging around you is making me question my belief that there are no coincidences," Tayanita mumbles to herself.

"You mean you think someone did this to me on purpose?" I let go with a cuss word as she applies the ice pack to a different area.

"Not unless you have some enemies I don't know about. I meant I know where your accident took place." She leads me to my favorite chair and moves the Ottoman so I can put my feet on it.

"How could you possibly know that?" I ask, feeling lost in the conversation.

"It's one of those things. You know, keeping it in the family — well, about the closest thing I have to family around here."

"Blue, I have no idea what you're talking about," I challenge with obvious exasperation.

"That's because it's not supposed to make sense to you. It's one of those weird coincidences. Mark's current fiancé's name is Shelby. She has a sister named Savannah. Savannah is engaged to a guy named Casey. Casey once owned a very popular upscale coffee shop called Tough Breaks."

"Small world theory at work, huh?" I wince as I shift

in the chair. "I should call and check on my sister. Rib pain sucks big time. I never realized breathing was like torture when you hurt your ribs. I should have been much more sympathetic toward Katie."

I try to slowly let out a breath. I'm not fooling anyone. Tayanita picks up on my discomfort right away.

"Are you sure you don't want me to take you to the ER? They'd probably give you something for pain."

"No, I don't want to mess with all of that. I think I probably just bruised something. I was more surprised than anything else. I'm sore, but it's nothing I can't handle. I've gotten worse injuries as a result of rough landings in the Huey."

"If you say so." Tayanita sighs. "I don't feel a broken rib, but I think you should probably still go to the doctor tomorrow to document your injuries in case someone finds the driver."

"Fat chance of that, I suppose. The police didn't seem hopeful. But, you're right about getting pictures and all that. I'll see about making an appointment tomorrow. Nothing against your profession, but I try to avoid all things medical. I've had enough poking and prodding to last a lifetime."

"I understand. Even I hate going to the doctor and I should know better. By the way, how did you get home? Why didn't you call me?"

"The police officer who responded called a cab for me. He wanted to call an ambulance, but I told him I would be okay."

"I wish you would have called me." I hear disappointment in her voice. My heart breaks a little. "It feels like you don't trust me to help you."

"I trust you just fine. I don't want to be a burden."

"Given all we've been through together, why would you even think that?" she asks with clear disbelief.

"It's complicated. To be honest, I was embarrassed to be caught in those circumstances. Every time I think I'm getting more self-sufficient, I seem to face a setback."

"John, you were hit by a car in a crosswalk. How is that your fault?"

"I know it sounds stupid, but I can't help but think if things were the way they used to be, I would've been able to see the car coming and jump out of the way. It's a little humiliating that I was the one who needed rescuing today."

"People with perfect vision get hit by cars too. I don't think you get to accept all the responsibility for this."

"I'm aware it's probably not rational, but the accident was the icing on the cake of a terrible day. I went to go try to find another job today. I never realized how inaccessible the world was until I became part of the society that needs special access. Blindness affects me in ways I never anticipated."

Corkscrew jumps up on my lap and curls up into a tight ball.

"Sorry, I think I've spoiled your baby," Tayanita remarks with a chuckle.

"It's okay. I could use a few extra snuggles today. Do you realize how many websites aren't compatible with screen readers? Graphics are cool, but they mess up the technology I count on. I had to ask someone to read me the job announcements. That doesn't do much to convince people I'm qualified to do a great job."

"That's on them, they need to make their materials more accessible to you," she argues.

"That's a nice argument in theory, but when I'm in the middle of a job search, it's kind of a moot point." I rub my eyes and scrub my hand down my face in frustration. "It wasn't only that. Even if I can find the right type of job to apply for, what do I say about my past employment?"

"You say you were a phenomenal member of the military with a spotless record, and you have tons of experience working as a team and being a supervisor."

"Uh-huh, I was so good at my job that I no longer have that job. I am sure that'll make perfect sense to a new employer."

"One of the first things you told me was that the governing board found you were not responsible. You need to believe that."

"Easier said than done," I mumble.

"Believe me, I know. In my mind, I have played, replayed and had a double feature of every single operation I've ever been involved in with a negative outcome. This includes the stupid freak accident that might someday kill me. Eventually, you have to move on and decide it is what it is. In your case, several dozen people have said it's not your fault."

"I know, but I was not the only person to pay a price for the incident. There were people under me who were demoted and I don't even know what happened to the pilot trainee. Last I heard, my marriage was not the only one to collapse under the stress of the investigation. That's a high price to pay because I let my ego get butt-hurt."

"Okay, let's for a moment argue everything you say is true, even though you have evidence to say it's not," Tayanita retorts.

"What if it is true? That's a question I'll never be able to answer. Because of the concussion, I don't even remember most of the day — just little pieces here and there. I only know the story because I've been able to piece it together through other people."

"That must be incredibly frustrating. I'm sorry," she replies gently. "But, even if everything you say is true, you said yourself the accident involved several things including a malfunction with your helicopter. You can't blame yourself for all of it."

"I feel like I'm spinning my wheels right now. I'm sorry I didn't call you. I knew you were slammed at work and I was embarrassed I even needed help."

"After all you've done for me, you never have to be embarrassed about asking for help. I would give it any time, any day, any way," Tayanita says emphatically.

Her simple statement is scary because I know it's true. Gathering my nerve, I decide to tell her the rest.

"I ran into another issue I wasn't sure how to get around," I admit.

"What do you mean?" Tayanita asks.

"Well, if I had called the hospital to ask for you, who would I say I was? I'm more than your friend and less than your partner."

"True."

"When we first started this idea of not naming what was between us, I thought I would be okay with that. But you've been practically living here for almost four months now. I don't think I'm comfortable with the rules we set up. I'd like to change the boundaries."

"Change the boundaries how?" Tayanita asks, her voice filled with fear.

"I'm ready to be more, whatever more means to you."

Tayanita walks behind my chair and bends down and kisses me in an awkward upside down kiss.

"I can't tell you how relieved I am to hear you say that. I made the same decision a couple weeks ago, but I wasn't sure how to tell you. I was afraid you wouldn't want to change the status quo."

"This is a heck of a way to figure it all out, but consider the status quo changed. When I'm feeling up to breathing without screaming in pain, let's celebrate."

"Sounds like a plan to me," Tayanita carefully hugs me as I lean in to kiss her.

# CHAPTER FIFTEEN

# TAYANITA

"*Etsi*, I don't understand, why are we even doing this?" Ketki asks, as she trudges along beside me.

It still warms my heart every time she uses the Cherokee word for mother. I've noticed it's something she's been doing a lot more often recently. Teenagers are funny, but I won't complain. I love it. It's like Shelby and I have different roles in her life but she's made room for both of us.

"Doing what?"

"Why am I spending my time with you on a nature walk? You realize this is Florida and it's hot outside?"

"I am aware. That's why it's early in the morning."

"All I'm saying is you could've come over and played video games with me and we could've slept in until noon. Besides, we would've had air conditioning."

"Come on, it's not that bad. I thought you liked being outside," I cajole.

"I also don't understand how come he has to come along. I don't know him," she argues.

"We're going on a hike together so you can get to

know him. John is an important person in my life. It feels silly of me to keep two people who are so important to me apart."

"What if he doesn't like any other girls except you? I don't know what to say to him. I have a hard enough time figuring out what to say to boys my own age. This is weird."

"Why is it so weird?" I ask, confused by her response. "You don't seem grossed out by Savannah and Casey or Jade and Declan."

Ketki chews on her bottom lip while she ponders what to say. "I'm not sure. It just is. I don't know if you'll be like my friend Joel's mom and dad. He used to live with his dad, but then his dad got a new girlfriend. They got married, and she became his stepmom. Suddenly, Joel had to go live with his grandparents because whoever this lady was decided she didn't like him very much. What if that happens? Maybe he doesn't like people with autism."

"First of all, John is a kind of person who likes all sorts of people. He even has a little sister he adores. I'm sure he'll think you're the bees-knees."

"I've never understood that saying. Bees don't have knees, and if they did, why are they so good?"

Her question makes me stop in the middle of the trail. "You know, I've never thought about it. You're right. I don't know why we say it. I guess that might've come from a cartoon. Some illustrator somewhere might have thought it was a good idea to draw a bee with kneecaps."

"That's weird," Ketki states flatly. "You know what else is weird?"

"What's weird?" I ask, playing along.

"Why are we taking a blind guy on a nature hike?

That seems silly. Well, silly and dangerous."

"You're not wrong. It's a little more dangerous than I'm used to. But, John and I have been hiking many times. You'll be surprised how easily he moves."

"But what's the point if he can't see things or take pictures along the way? Doesn't he get bored?" Ketki presses in her usual way of asking a thousand and one questions.

"That's our job. We're here to be his eyes for him and let him know what we see and how it makes us feel."

"Okay, then it's even more weird," Ketki protests.

"What do you mean?"

"My science teacher says no two people view the world exactly the same way. So, if you and I are telling him what something looks like, how is he going to know which one is right?"

"John has an advantage — I guess you could call it — over some people who are blind. He only lost his sight a few years ago. He has a strong memory of how things looked during the time he could still see."

"Do you think it makes him sad? I would be sad. I would wonder if the things in the world were still as pretty as I remember them."

"I don't know. I haven't asked him, but you're correct, it would probably be frustrating to remember what something looks like, but not be able to see it. As a mom, I think I would miss seeing my daughter's face."

"Do you think it would be rude of me to ask him?" Ketki asks. "Some people tell me I ask way too many questions."

"Well, I probably wouldn't start up a conversation

that way, but John is very open about being blind. I don't think he would mind answering a few questions as long as you're polite."

"Yeah, I know what you mean. Some people are ignorant about my autism, especially if I'm nervous and my hands are flapping. Sometimes, people think I do it on purpose. We had a substitute teacher the other day who thought I was doing it to get attention. I almost ended up in the principal's office because I tried to say something and stand up for myself. I don't want to be like this, I just am."

"You're right Ketki, that was rude. She shouldn't have said that regardless of whether she is a teacher or not. I don't think John will be that way. He's a very cool guy."

As we go around the corner, I see John sitting on a bench soaking up the sun. When I look closer, I realize he has his headphones on and must be listening to the audiobook I got him the other day.

I walk over and stand in front of him. When my presence blocks out the sun, he opens his eyes and grins.

"That didn't take long," he comments.

"I had to go to the parking lot to get Ki from Mark." I turn to Ketki and instruct, "Are you going to introduce yourself?"

She steps forward. "I know most people shake hands, but that kinda weirds me out. Is it okay if I don't shake your hand? My name is Ketki Littleson."

"That's all right, Ketki. Shaking hands can be a tad awkward for me too. So... we'll skip it and say we did it anyway," John answers. "I'm John Ashford, a friend of your mom's."

"Did *Etsi* tell you she used to be in love with my dad? That's okay because now she's not anymore. Now Shelby loves my dad," Ketki asserts.

John chuckles. "As a matter of fact, Tayanita told me all about you. It was one of the first things we ever talked about."

"Did she tell you about the icky parts too?"

John seems a little stunned by the question, but gamely tries to answer, "Yep, she told me the hard parts too."

"Did you get mad? Sometimes I still get mad at her. But I try not to be."

"That's understandable. We can't judge the decisions other people make unless we've walked in their shoes. However, I suppose her choices may not seem to make any sense to you. But here is a little secret ... sometimes our choices don't make sense to the grown-ups either. We all just do the best we can."

"I know. But sometimes I forget and it still hurts."

"I understand. I've made choices in my life I wish I could make over again. But unfortunately, life doesn't work that way."

"What do you wish you could do differently?" Ketki asks with open curiosity.

John leans forward on the bench and runs his hand through his hair. "Well, if I had a time machine, I would go back to the morning before the accident, the one that cost me my sight. I would go back and double check all my work to make sure the accident didn't happen. But, the real world isn't like a magical place. I can't do that, so I'm learning to cope with being different," John explains.

"You're not the only person who's different. I have autism. Some people say that's weird, but other people say it's good because it makes me good at things like computer games. So, I'm not sure if I would want my autism to go away."

"I thought you said —" I interrupt, thinking back to the conversation we just had.

"I meant that part for my hand flaps, I like being smart and able to solve problems. I especially like programming my computer to do anything I want it to do. Sometimes, being different is fun."

"I've never thought of it that way. Great perspective."

"Why are you doing things that are hard to do when you're blind?" Ketki blurts.

John sighs as he ponders her question for a moment. "I guess I keep doing hard things because I don't want to give up. I like to go hiking with your mom because I love to be outside. I miss doing a lot of things. I used to climb rocks and go down into caves. I like to collect different things from my travels. Even though it's harder now, I still like to be outside. Sometimes, I'd like to pretend I am not blind and things are like they were before I got hurt."

"I think I understand. I like to collect things too. Sometimes the things I collect have dirt and slimy stuff all over them. I hate getting my hands dirty. But, I like collecting stones and feathers so much I try to forget about the dirt and do it anyway."

"Did your mom tell you anything about me?" John asks.

"Not much," Ketki answers. "Only that she was excited about going on a date with you."

"Well, I'm relieved. It would've been bad if she wasn't excited," John responds in an amused voice. "But, I was thinking more of the fact I used to study rocks in college. As a former pilot, I know quite a bit about birds too. I guess you could say I'm into stones and feathers too."

Ketki swings her head around to look at me as she asks, "Is this true? He's not saying this to be a fake friend, is he? I've had that happen before."

"I know, but John is telling the truth. I saw his transcript. His grades were better than mine," I tease.

"Okay, I had to check to be safe."

"My sister would be impressed with your safety instincts. She teaches teenagers all that stuff about safety because she's a cop. It's good for you to be cautious."

"Tayanita, have you met his family? Are they nice people?"

"Yes, Ketki. The Ashford's are very lovely people."

"Your mom even gets along with my sister now. When my sister first heard I was dating somebody, she was a little nervous for me. But, your mom has done a good job of making friends with her."

"Hey, it's not just me. Your sister is cool," I insist.

"Do you need to know anything else, Ketki?" John asks gently. "I like your mom quite a bit and I want you to feel comfortable."

"I'm sorry I'm being weird about this, but my Aunt Savannah had to go to court a bunch of times to face down people who tried to hurt her. I don't want that to happen to my mom."

"I don't want anything bad to happen to your mom

either. I like her lots," John admits.

"That's good. It would be weird if my mom introduced me to somebody who didn't like her," Ketki answers.

"That is true. I haven't been rock-hounding since a few months before my accident. Would you like to help me figure out a way to do it now?"

"I'm good at categorizing rocks and feathers. Maybe we could sort them and you could try to guess them based on their texture and weight," Ketki challenges.

John scratches the back of his neck before he answers, "I don't know. It's been a while. I don't know if that'll be enough information for me to make a guess."

"You're silly! If you get stuck, I'll describe the rock and give you hints. It'll be part of the game, almost like it's a scavenger hunt."

"Something tells me you'll probably be better at this game than I am."

Ketki shrugs. "That's okay, I'm always better at the games I play than everyone else. I'm used to it by now. Usually, I still have fun though."

John snickers. "Well, it's a good thing you don't have a problem with overconfidence. Let's go see if we can do this. Who knows? I might be better than you think."

"Umm-hmm, that's what they all say," Ketki rolls her eyes dramatically and puts her elbow out for John to grab.

John groans. "I am so out of shape. I can't believe one little hike made me feel like I finished the New York

Marathon."

"Have you done it?"

"Have I done what?" John asks as he rolls his shoulder to stretch out his muscles.

"Run any marathons? I'm a big runner, but I guess I didn't realize you might be too."

"Add that to my list of things I used to do. I used to run a lot as part of my fitness regime. If I was deployed near a marathon, I would usually join in. Josselyn and I used to train together. She is a huge fitness buff."

"Do you miss it? I'd go a little stir crazy if I couldn't run."

"Why is this the first time we've ever talked about this? We've been together for months. I had no idea running was this important to you."

"I don't know. I guess I don't talk about my running very much. I don't have many people in my life who think jogging is fun, so I do it on my own during my lunch hours at work or after work if I've had a stressful day."

"Given the big workout Ketki gave me today, I'm surprised she doesn't run with you."

"Ketki is one of the people in my life who doesn't understand the whole concept of running. She is not a big fan of sweat in general, so she sees no point."

"I do miss it. I'd like to be able to run again. If today is any indication, I'm gonna have to build up my strength to keep up with your daughter."

"Yeah, once she got over her fear of you, she was unstoppable," I say with a laugh. "Lay on the bed, I'll give you a back rub."

"Okay, whatever you say. If you can make me feel

better, I'm all over that," John says as he stretches out on the bed. "That rope and pulley system she rigged up for us was genius. It saved me from some dicey situations today. I bet that would work for jogging too."

"The thing I notice when I play video games with Ketki is she is good at solving problems. I'm so proud of the way she acted today."

"I didn't expect to do as much talking as we did on our nature hike," John admits.

"I imagine not. Ketki can be a little overwhelming sometimes, but you handled it like a champ."

"It took some time to get used to the unusual way she asks questions, but her questions were often insightful. I think she's great."

"Clearly, she thought you're awesome too. I couldn't have hoped this meeting between the two of you would go any better. I'm so pleased."

"Tayanita, I'm blind. I didn't turn into some weird troll who eats children. I love kids. Part of my duties with the Coast Guard was to go to schools and talk to kids about a future in the military. Some of my colleagues didn't like that part of the job, but it was my favorite part. There's something about seeing the hope in their faces."

"I didn't mean it like that. Ketki can be funny about the people she lets into her life. I'm glad you are one of the people she thinks is okay."

John quickly rolls over, almost dislodging me from where I'm perched straddling his backside. As we are face-to-face, he reaches up and strokes my face.

"What about you? What do you think of me — of us?"

I lean down to kiss him. "Obviously, I think you are a little more than okay. Meeting you has changed my life."

"It's safe to say my life has changed for the better because you are in it, and I'm not just saying that because you give the world's best massages," John adds as he reaches up and pulls me back for another kiss.

"Well, I should hope not. I am a woman of many talents," I quip.

Sitting upright, still straddling John, I announce, "I don't know exactly when it happened, but somewhere along the way, you helped me remember I am more than the choices I've made in the past. I love you for that."

"Is that all you love me for?" John teases.

"No, there's so much more. I could tell you all about it, but it might take days."

"In that case, give me the cliff notes version. I have a few ideas how we could better spend our time."

"By all means, tell me your stellar ideas."

John reaches out and grabs a couple handfuls of my hair as he pulls me closer. "I think I'd rather show you."

"Mmm ... that works too," I mumble as I wonder how I got so lucky.

# Chapter Sixteen

# John

When I was a kid, one of my biggest ambitions was to stay home and do whatever I wished, whenever I wanted to. Like many things in childhood, the fantasy is far better than the reality.

Sure, the first few days were great, but after Katie got out of the hospital, my days have fallen into a deep pit of mundaneness. Even my family is getting a little sick of me hanging around. My sister told me to get a life because I needed to butt out of hers; my mom has hinted I might be wearing out my welcome. It appears my presence in her life is interfering with her afternoon soaps.

To be blunt, I'm bored out of my mind. I've discovered daytime television is insufferably monotonous, computer games are difficult to play when you can't see, and once you've seen a football game once or twice, they lose a little something. I've started waiting for Tayanita to come home from work like I'm some high-strung puppy with separation anxiety.

She has been great about it. In all truth, she's far more understanding than she probably should be. I am even annoying myself these days.

We spend a lot of time wandering around the state parks. She also found us a virtually deserted running path. I'm getting my muscle tone back again and feel like the athlete I once was.

As I finish washing the dishes from breakfast, my phone rings.

"Go for John," I answer.

"Uh … um, this is Ketki."

"Oh, hi Ketki. Your mom's not here. She's at work."

"I know. That's why I'm calling. *Etsi* said to tell you her phone battery was about to go dead, but she has two back-to-back surgeries."

"Wow! That's a lot. She worked last night too."

"I know that too. But, she doesn't listen to me when I tell her that she's working too hard."

"Is there anything I can help you with?" I offer hesitantly. I don't know Ketki well, and I don't know how much I can do for her if she actually needs help. This is not a place I'm comfortable being. I like to be the one in charge with all the answers.

"I don't know. How much do you know about math?"

"Enough to graduate from flight school at the top of my class."

"Sounds good. You've been drafted to be my tutor for the day since mom has to work."

"So, where should we study?"

"Mom usually takes me out to eat."

"Okay, I can always eat. Where would you like to go?"

"Mom and I always go to this pizza joint next to her house. They have good food and big tables for doing work."

"It's a date. How about I meet you about one o'clock? I'll take the bus to Tayanita's place and figure it out from there."

"You live halfway between my dad's house and Tayanita's house. My dad can stop by and pick you up."

"Ketki, I don't know if you forgot I'm dating your mom. I like her a lot. She likes me too, and I'm not sure your dad is okay with that."

"You don't get it, John. It's a great thing for my dad if you fall in love with my mom."

"I don't know if he'll see it that way. You know, it's kind of a guy thing."

"My dad is cool. You'll see."

"This may be the most insane idea I've ever had," I mutter to myself as I tuck in my shirt.

I take a deep breath as I push the button on the intercom to my front door. "I'll be right there, Ketki."

I'm not sure why I feel like I am a teenager about to go out on my first date. For some reason, even though Mark and Tayanita are not an item anymore, it seems important for us to get along. I can't imagine what I would do if the shoe were on the other foot. Fortunately, Josselyn has never asked for my approval of anyone she's dated. I'm not sure how I'd respond to that.

I scoop Corkscrew off the ground to prevent him from going outside as I open the door.

"You never told me you had a cat!" Ketki exclaims.

"I suppose that's because you've never asked me. This is Corkscrew."

"Did you know in Japan, orange cats are considered bad luck — sort of like black cats are here?" Ketki comments.

"No, I didn't know that. Corkscrew here is a lucky cat though."

"Can I hold him?"

"Okay, put your hand on my arm so I know where you are before we try the handoff. The kitten loves people, but he doesn't like being held up in the air," I instruct.

"I'll be careful, I promise."

"Ketki, if the cat doesn't like being up in the air, maybe it would be better if you sat down," interjects Mark.

"That's a good idea. See that big brown chair over there? That's Corkscrew's favorite chair. Why don't we go over there?"

As I carefully make my way into the living room while I'm holding the kitten, I hear Ketki say, "See Dad, I told you we can work out anything between us because John and I figured out a way to hike."

Mark sounds incredibly embarrassed as he responds, "Ketki, my nervousness isn't all about John having a visual impairment. I ask to meet everyone you hang out with."

"That's true. It's a little embarrassing because I'm a teenager now. I should be able to pick my own friends," Ketki argues.

"Sorry, I agree with your dad on this one. It never hurts to have a second opinion. Wait until you meet my sister Katie. She'll tell you all sorts of embarrassing stories about how I used to screen her friends. I considered it my duty as her big brother. In fact, I still do that even though she's a grown up. That's what you do for people you love."

"I know you guys are probably right, but it still feels weird because some of my friends don't have to do this."

"Well, I consider it a privilege to be a pain in your butt if it keeps you safe," Mark responds.

"Okay, I get it. When I worked with the police and helped Aunt Savannah, I learned more than I ever needed to know about total creeps."

Ketki reaches out and takes Corkscrew from my arms as she sits down in the chair. It's obvious he has decided Ketki is a cat person. He begins purring loudly, like he does when Tayanita holds him.

"Katie would be so proud of you. She lectures teenagers all the time on Internet safety. You seem to have learned those lessons already."

"She's the one who is a police officer, right?"

"I only have one sister, and she is proud to be a police officer."

"Wait," Mark interrupts. "Officer Ashford is your sister? The DA told me she was injured on the job, is she going to be okay?"

Now, it's my turn to look at him suspiciously. "How do you know my sister?" I ask gruffly.

"Whoa!" Mark answers with a chuckle. "You can put away your big brother card. Your sister was a witness for me in a recent case. That's the only reason the DA even brought her up."

"I always figured you would be on the opposite side of the police," I answer candidly.

"Sometimes I am, but a lot of times I work with them," Mark explains.

"Good to know," I add lamely. I have now officially run out of things to say to Mark and don't know where to take the conversation from here.

After a few moments of stifling silence, Mark clears his throat. "Let's stop pretending and get this over with, okay?"

"I don't know if I can do that. It depends on what I'm agreeing to," I answer with an edge to my voice.

Mark sighs. "Look, I know this is awkward. I'm sorry about that. Nita may be my ex, but she's still the mother of my child. We were best friends before we were spouses and I don't think there will ever be a day that I don't look out for her well-being. Are you going to have a problem with that?"

"I suppose it depends on how closely you're going to watch out for her," I answer tersely.

"Well, I won't be knocking on your bedroom window or anything. I want you to know I'm watching her back though," Mark replies.

I breathe a sigh of relief. "I suspect you think I'll have a problem with that. Surprisingly, I don't. From what Tayanita has told me about your relationship, I wouldn't expect you to do anything less."

"Good. So we're clear, Ketki and Shelby are the most important people in my life. Nita ranks right up there too because, without her, I wouldn't have Ketki. If you do anything to hurt Ketki or Tayanita, I will hunt you down and probably hurt you."

"Understood. It's not my intention to hurt either one of them. Tayanita and I may have met in an unconventional manner, but she's quickly become the most important person in my life."

Mark slaps me on the back of the shoulder. "Best of luck. Tayanita can be challenging, but she deserves happiness. If you're the guy to bring it to her, more power to you."

I am a little startled by the sudden end of the Inquisition. Frankly, I expected much worse. "Uh … Okay," I stammer. "Thanks, I guess. I think it will mean a lot to Tayanita to know you support our relationship."

"Are you guys done circling each other like stray dogs in a parking lot? I'm hungry, and I've got math homework to do. So, can we get all this guy bonding stuff over with?"

I smile at her. "As far as I'm concerned, I've said what I need to. I want your mom and you in my life."

"You don't care that I'm different?" Ketki asks tentatively.

"I don't care about your differences, if you don't care about mine," I respond.

"I don't know what to say," Ketki admits, "It's not exactly true to say I don't care that you can't see. I wish you could see. It would be fun to go rock hounding with you and show you what I see."

"Ketki, I don't think you would be human if you didn't feel that way sometimes. We'll have to work around my visual impairment. It's a reality of my life now."

"I think I can do that. I was good at figuring out what we needed to do when we went hiking."

"You were. Did your mom tell you we've been using your system when I run with her?"

"That's like the best news ever. Maybe now she'll stop bugging me to go with her. Did she tell you I don't like running?"

"She did. You never know, maybe we'll change your mind."

"Don't hold your breath. I would rather spend my time programming a computer. I can't figure out why my mom likes to run from one spot to another and then back. It makes no sense."

Mark laughs. "Ketki, that's probably the first of many things people do that you won't understand."

"Duh, Dad, tell me something I don't know," Ketki responds. Her tone reminds me so much of Katie's; I can almost envision her defiant body language and eye roll.

"Ketki, do you still read time on a regular clock?"

"Of course. Why would you ask that?"

"I have a weird story for you. I went out to eat the other day and was trying to explain to the waiter how he could best help me, but he didn't know how to read anything except a digital clock. That wasn't much help to me."

"I think that's stupid. You learn how to tell time when you're in kindergarten. So, why did you need him to know how to tell time?" Ketki asks.

"When you place things in front of me, I need you

to pretend you're looking at the face of a clock. I am right-handed, so I like to have my drink at two o'clock. Usually, if there is a salad or something, I ask you to put it at noon."

"Oh! I get it. So, your silverware would be at nine o'clock and three o'clock, right?"

"Exactly! You're quick. If you put something new in front of me, if you could tell me like this, 'There are breadsticks at eleven o'clock.', I would appreciate it."

"That makes so much more sense now. After I met you the other day, I went home and put a blindfold on to see what it would be like to be you. I spilled my breakfast cereal all over because I kept bumping it."

"That was a cool thing for you to do. Not very many people try to put themselves in my shoes."

"Yeah, I wish people would understand more about what it's like to have autism."

"Can you tell me what you mean?"

"Okay, this'll sound dumb, but my friends at school like to play with makeup and all these weird lotions and stuff. That kind of stuff completely grosses me out. I don't like the way it feels on my skin. You should see me in the summer when I have to wear sunscreen. Even though I need to wear it, it's still hard. It's like my body can feel every molecule of it. My brain thinks it's bad, like crushed glass. Sometimes, it's hard to concentrate on the things I'm supposed to concentrate on because I'm so busy thinking about everything else."

"I can see why that would be frustrating."

"Is there something about being blind you hate more than anything?"

"Well, it makes me sad I can't see you and your mom. It was frustrating for me when I knew my sister was hurt, but I couldn't see for myself if she was doing better. I had to rely on other things like the sound of her breathing and whether she makes noises as if she's in pain to figure out how she's feeling."

"That sounds hard too."

"You know one of the small things that bug me about being blind is having to use my cane. It makes me feel awkward and clumsy."

"Why don't you get a dog like Hope? Hope and Lexicon are like the coolest dogs ever."

"Are they seeing-eye dogs?" I ask, confused about what she's talking about.

"No, Hope and Lexicon help find missing people. But, my friend Mitch has this place where he trains all sorts of dogs. You should talk to him to see if he could help you get a dog. I saw something on National Geographic about seeing-eye dogs and how helpful they are to people. I bet you would like a dog more than a white cane."

It takes a couple of moments for the puzzle pieces to fall into place. "Ketki, is this place called Hope's Haven? Is there a woman who works there named Zoe?"

"Yes! How did you know? Zoe has the coolest hair ever. It's so long and a pretty color. She always looks like a fashion model. I tried to talk my mom into letting me do that, but she said because I have dark hair like she does, the hair dye wouldn't show up unless I bleach my hair and she says I am too young to do that."

"Your mom is probably right. One time when my sister was a teenager, she tried to dye her hair green for

St. Patrick's Day. It did not go well. Katie's scalp broke out in a very bad rash. Then, her hair fell out. She had to wear a hat for months."

"Oh, that sucks. I bet the kids made fun of her."

"I tried to stop that from happening, but you know how kids are."

"Do you know Zoe?" Ketki asks.

"No, but I met her brother. He was dating my sister, but I don't know if they are still a thing."

"Why? Did they break up?"

"It looks like they might have. He wasn't too happy my sister got shot."

"That's rude! It's not like your sister told the bullets where to go. I've met a bunch of police officers and I know their job is dangerous. Did he not get a clue? Boys are so stupid!"

I laugh as I respond, "I don't know the whole story. If that's what he thought, I agree with you; he's stupid. My sister is completely awesome."

"I can't wait to meet her. Do you think she would be sad if you went to go talk to Mitch about getting a helper dog?"

"No, I don't think she would be sad at all. She was excited about the idea."

"The next time I have a sleepover at Mom's, I'll ask her if she can introduce you to Jessica and Mitch."

"That sounds like an excellent plan. Speaking of plans ... aren't we supposed to be doing your math homework?"

Ketki's sighs as she responds, "I was hoping you

might forget about that and focus on the pizza."

"Sorry. I can't do that; I promised your dad I would take good care of you, including the tough stuff."

Ketki shuffles things around in her backpack for a while. Finally, she taps me on the forearm. "I don't know how this is going to work. You can't see my paper or my math book."

I pull my portable reader out of my own backpack and hold it up for her to see. I put my headphones on and plug them into the little pen-like device.

"What in the world is that?" she asks in a curious voice.

"It's a portable scanner that reads text out loud to me."

"Oh! That's totally cool. My friend Tristan is a software programmer. He has worked with optical character recognition stuff before. He uses it mostly for law enforcement stuff. He was telling me sometimes the computer can pick up similarities in handwriting the human eye might miss."

"So, I don't have to explain to you what this does?" I ask.

"Nope, I have that part figured out. But, I do want to try it to see what it's like, is that okay?"

"Sure. Why don't you show me the problem you're stuck on?" I offer.

Ketki's voice sounds brighter. "Okay. I put my math paper at six o'clock. The problem is about halfway down the page."

Scanning the page slowly, I listen to the device read out what's on the page. "Ketki, did you mean this to be a two or a five? Sometimes, this thing has a little trouble with handwriting."

"It says twenty-two," she responds.

"It's been a while since I've been in Algebra II, but I don't think you can solve for the square root of two. Isn't it an irrational number?"

Ketki snatches her paper back. "I can't believe I thought it was way more complicated. I made a stupid multiplication error."

"Ketki, it's not a problem. Everybody makes mistakes," I say when I hear her becoming distressed.

"But, I shouldn't make mistakes in math. It's my best subject."

"Trust me; I know what it's like to make a mistake at the thing you do best. But sometimes it just happens."

"John, do you have to leave because you helped me figure this out?"

"I'm here for you all afternoon. If you get done with your homework, I've got a chess game on my iPad. I have a feeling you'll give me a run for my money."

Ketki clicks her tongue. "I would love to play chess. Dad says out of fairness, I have to tell new opponents I'm scary good."

"That is the best news I've heard all day. I can never find anybody to play chess with. People tend to get upset when I win all the time."

"OMG! I thought people only got that way with me. You're on, John. You don't mind losing to a girl, right?"

"As long as you don't cheat, bring it on. If you beat me fair and square, you get to wear the badge of honor with pride."

"Wouldn't it be funny if we actually had a trophy to pass back-and-forth?"

"I'll tell you what — you beat me at chess and I will get you your trophy."

"Did anybody tell you I am as smart and stubborn as my mom? You are so going down. I'm not even going to feel bad about it," Ketki says with confidence.

I hold up my glass of root beer. "Shall we toast to the best person winning?"

She taps her glass against mine and says, "Absolutely. Let the butt-kicking begin."

# Chapter Seventeen

# Tayanita

"Are you ready to grab some coffee? I don't know about you, but I am exhausted. Those kids had so many questions today. You were amazingly patient with them," Shelby asks me as she places her arm around my shoulder and escorts me out of her office. "I can't thank you enough."

"I was surprised how many people were part of the seminar. It was a lot more than the last time we did this. Did you recruit every student you teach?"

"I didn't do anything special. I guess my students heard about how much fun your presentations are from the last group of kids who went through. They all share a community bulletin board."

"Their reaction surprises me because I kind of shot from the hip about what it was like to be in my job. I was completely winging it."

"You wing well because the kids ate up every word you said."

"I guess I'm passionate about what I do," I admit. "It's easy to become jaded after a while. Seeing their excitement over the possibility of working in the medical field is a refreshing change for me. It's been a long time since someone has been so excited about what I do."

"I don't know about that; I was excited the day you stopped me from having a panic attack before my surgery. As I recall, I kinda thought you were the best thing since sliced bread. Come to think of it, my opinion of you has changed little."

"Stop with the compliments unless you're willing to take a few of your own," I tease, knowing Shelby doesn't like to have anyone point out that she is exceptionally talented or nice. "You're starting to sound like John. Every time I turn around, the man has something phenomenally gracious to say about me. I'm getting a little self-conscious."

"You want to talk about it? I don't want to be nosy. Oh, never mind, I want to be nosy. I can't even lie and tell you I'm not interested. I am totally, completely, and insanely curious."

"Why?" I ask with trepidation.

Shelby slips a cup of coffee in front of me and slides onto the barstool beside me. She shrugs. "I don't know. Maybe it's because I'm a little sister and I'm prone to be curious about other people's business. Or it might be because I miss Savannah and Casey. They are doing great in California, but it's too far away for my taste. Ketki talks about John all the time. I guess I'd rather hear about him from you."

I twist the ends of my hair and tie it up into a ponytail as I think about my options. Finally, I shake my head. "I'm not sure when this happened, but somehow you've gone from being my arch-nemesis to one of my few friends. So, I guess if I'm going to talk about it with anybody, it should probably be you."

"That sounds serious. Is there something wrong?"

"No," I insist. "If anything, things are going a little too well."

"What do you mean, 'too well'?"

"After things didn't work out between Mark and me, I figured I would be alone for the rest of my life. I felt that was what I deserved for having left Mark and Ketki."

"I know we've talked about this before. Postpartum depression is a real thing. It's as real as the cancer cells that were eating away at my skin. If you wouldn't blame me for my cancer, why would you blame yourself for postpartum depression?"

"I don't know. You would think I would know better with my medical training. However, sometimes I can't seem to get that message from my brain to my heart."

"Sometimes, you have to let go of the past and forgive yourself for what you weren't able to do."

"I try, but —"

"No but. Since you came back into Ketki's life, you've stepped up. You could have been bitter and angry at the relationship between Mark and me, but you weren't. You allowed him to move on with his life and fall in love with me. In my book, that makes you exceptional."

"It would've been wrong to stand in the way of Mark's chance at happiness," I argue stubbornly.

"Exactly. So … why isn't it wrong for you to stand in the way of happiness because you think you need to pay some penance for what you've done before? Life doesn't work that way. You do the best you can with what you know, and then everyone makes up the rest."

"Is it that easy to forget about all the mistakes I made before?"

"Probably not. Ketki is happy and healthy and has a great relationship with you now. What is the point in hanging on to what you did a decade ago? You have so many more positive things in your life. Why not focus on them?"

Her question makes me catch my breath. Could it be as easy as choosing to focus on new things?

"You're right. My life is great right now. I have a man who loves everything about me — even the ugly stuff. I have a great job I adore, and my relationship with Ketki is better than I ever dreamed it could be."

"See? That's what I'm saying. Dwelling on the past won't fix anything in your future."

"Speaking of not moving on with your future, is everything all right with you?"

Shelby takes a long drink of her coffee and studies me carefully. "I don't even know if I have the right to say anything because of what's going on with you."

"What do you mean what's going on with me? I told you I am as happy as I've ever been in my whole life."

"What about what happened with the incident at your work?"

My mouth opens in shock. "Didn't Ketki tell you?"

"Obviously not."

"Last week, I got the all clear. There was no transmission of the HIV to me. I guess you're stuck with me for a while — at least until Ketki goes to college. At the rate she's going, that might be in a couple of years."

"I know. Ketki is exceptionally smart. It was one of

the first things I noticed about her."

"It's obvious you love my ex-husband and my daughter, so what's going on?" I press, remembering my conversation with Mark.

Shelby gets up and paces around her kitchen. She stops and turns toward me as she admits, "I'm afraid I am going to die."

"What? Have you had a reoccurrence of your skin cancer?" I ask with alarm.

Shelby leans on the counter. "No, thank goodness. It's this weird thing in my head. I know it's totally weird, but things are so great with Mark and me right now, I'm afraid to jinx it."

"I know what you mean. Maybe it's time for you to let go of some of your past too."

"You're right, this is hard," Shelby says with a wry chuckle. "I know Mark would marry me yesterday if I told him I was ready."

"He is not the only one. Ketki already considers you to be her mom. You might as well make it official."

"Maybe that's part of the problem. Now that you are so closely intertwined with our lives, I don't want to take that position away from you," Shelby says.

"Shelby, you can't change the fact that I am Ketki's mother. Whether you have a wedding worthy of one of those goofy reality shows or you decide to stay engaged, I am still Ketki's mom. A piece of paper doesn't change that."

"So, you don't mind that Ketki calls me Mom?" Shelby asks. "Maybe I misread it, but I always thought our relationship was difficult for you."

"I have struggled. I won't lie. However, Ketki and I seem to have reached a compromise quite by accident. She calls me *Etsi*, which is the Cherokee word for mother. She likes spending time with me, but she considers you to be her primary mother figure. Honestly, I think that's probably how it should be. You've been in her life longer than I have at this point."

"I've never thought about it that way, but I guess it's true," Shelby concedes.

"So, if that's the reason you are holding back, please don't. Ketki wants you guys to be married. Mark has made no secret of his intentions. I am working on forgiving myself for the mistakes I've made and moving on with my life so I can have a healthier relationship with Ketki."

"I hope you don't feel like you have to step back if Mark and I get married. That's not what we want at all."

At that moment, something deep in my soul cracks open. Although I haven't been able to describe my fears well, Shelby inadvertently addressed them. As much as I know Mark and Shelby's relationship is the best thing for Ketki, my secret fear has always been that once they figure out their relationship and settle down, I would be excluded. I know that sounds irrational since for almost a decade I eliminated myself from Ketki's life. I don't have an explanation for it except I am in a very different place now.

I take a deep breath as I try to explain, "No, that's not what I meant at all. I have no intention of going anywhere. I won't abandon Ketki again. Thanks to John, I am well on my way to figuring out who I am these days as opposed to who I once was. I plan to be involved in my daughter's life as long as she is comfortable having me there."

"Ketki is going to be so happy. I think she worries about that a lot. Perhaps we can make it easier for her if we get this all sorted out." Shelby comes over and gives me a hug. "I'm so glad we finally sat down and talked this through. It sounds like Mark and I need to do some talking."

"You're not the only one. I need to figure out where John and I stand. I need to develop a little courage and faith that things are as good as they seem to be. I'm afraid to hope."

"Please bring John by. I'd love to meet him. I'd like to meet the man who makes you smile," Shelby says with a slightly soggy grin. "I'd like to thank him for seeing the stunning woman you are."

As I walk into the place that feels more like home than my own house, I smell something tantalizing. When I walk into the kitchen, I'm greeted with the devastatingly sexy image of my partner standing in worn jeans and an apron.

I purposely drop my purse on the sideboard with a loud thud.

John turns in my direction. "You're just in time for dinner. I hope you don't mind, I skipped the candles. I wasn't sure I wouldn't be clumsy and burn the house down."

"You know, it's funny. I feel the same way around candles. When I was a child, I tipped one of my mom's candles and spilled the wax on myself. Ever since then, I've been a little leery of them. So, having no candles works fine for me." I walk over to the stove and lift the lid. "What are we having?"

"I made Swedish meatballs," John announces with pride. "I found an audiobook version of a cookbook. For me, that works better than listening to television shows. I can never quite tell what the chef is doing when I watch those shows. However, the instructions in the audiobook were clear."

"However you pulled it off, it looks phenomenal."

John blushes. "Thank you. By the way, I have you to thank for this."

"Me? What did I do?" I carry the pan over to the table.

"I don't know if I can fully explain this, but helping you overcome the challenges in your life has given me motivation to stretch my own boundaries and tackle things I'm afraid of. You can't give me back my sight, probably no one can. But you've given me the sense of freedom and adventure I was afraid I'd lost."

"I don't know if I've done all that much. I drug you along on a few nature hikes and made myself at home here so you would have to feed me. I don't know if that makes me heroic or a moocher."

"In my book, it makes you an epic hero. You helped me change my perspective from what I could no longer do to what is possible. It's priceless."

"Okay, if you say so, but I still think I've come out ahead in this deal. I was just telling Shelby how much better my life is with you in it."

"What did she have to say?" John asks.

"I thought it would be an awkward conversation

given the fact we both once loved Mark, yet, it wasn't. It was almost as if we were both waiting for each other to give permission for our lives to move on. At some point in today's conversation, I figured out I always had the permission, I've simply never used it."

"So what does that mean?" John starts to eat.

"I guess the upshot of it all is Shelby and I have been carrying around a lot of guilt for different reasons. Now, it seems like we both can let the guilt go. I can move forward in life without fear of losing the connection I have established with Ketki. I can't tell you how grateful I am for that. It's a gift I never expected to receive. When I left all those years ago, I never dreamed I would be in the spot I am today. I'm happy with Ketki and I am amazingly content with you."

"Content?" John challenges. "I want to be more than the feeling you get after Thanksgiving dinner."

"I'm sorry, I'm not doing a very good job of explaining this. Before I met you, you could probably tell I was unraveling at the edges. I tried to pretend everything was okay in my life. However, the truth was I was lost. I knew I had overcome the depression that drove the choices I made when I was younger; however, I was afraid to reach out and connect with people because I was fearful I might disappoint people again."

John reaches across the table and I grab his hand. "It always baffles me you don't see yourself as the strong, independent, capable, loving and beautiful person you are."

"I'm starting to be brave enough to see myself through your eyes. I know, it's ironic, isn't it? You can't see me, yet somehow you manage to see the real me under all my fears and insecurities. I want to see myself through your eyes because your vision of me is incredible. That's what I mean by content and settled. It's not a bad thing. It isn't."

"That goes both ways, you know," John replies. "I've changed my own perception of what I'm capable of simply because you believe I am capable of anything, regardless of my ability to see."

"From my perspective, I haven't seen much you can't do."

"So, what's next?" John asks.

"Funny you should ask. You've met Ketki and Mark, how would you like to meet everyone else?"

"Will you be by my side?"

"Absolutely, I don't plan to be anywhere else."

"Okay, I'm game if you are. Let's do this."

"I'm so glad, because I already told Shelby we would be at her barbecue on Saturday. It may feel a bit like being tossed in with the wolves, but I swear everyone there is rooting for us."

"Speaking of being thrown to the wolves, I got an interesting call from the Veterans' Administration while you were gone. I don't know what's going on, but the case manager wants me to come in for a meeting on Thursday."

"I can't imagine that would mean anything but good things. We are on a roll. It simply has to be positive news," I declare.

"As my grandmother used to say, 'From your lips to God's ears'."

# CHAPTER EIGHTEEN

# JOHN

HE'S NERVOUS. THAT'S THE impression I have of the guy in front of me. His hand was sweaty when he shook mine and his speech pattern is unusually fast. What I can't figure out is why he's nervous; I'm the one with no job even after months of looking.

The shuffling of paper seems to go on forever. I move forward in my seat. "Mr. Holmes, why are we here today?"

"Lieutenant Ashford, I don't know quite how to say this, but it appears our agency owes you an apology."

My mind races as I try to figure out what he's talking about. This place is a subcontractor of the Veterans' Administration. They're in charge of helping people like me find work. Technically speaking, the job matches have been less than ideal, but I can't complain because I met Tayanita through my totally crappy job.

"I hesitate to ask, but what do you have to apologize for?"

Edwin Holmes clears his throat before he responds in a diplomatic voice, "It has come to our attention we did not have complete documentation regarding your work history and education when we placed you in your previous positions."

"I tried to tell you over a year ago, but no one would listen."

"Yes, in reviewing your file I do see you tried to talk to our employment counselor about your history. But you need to understand many people who come into our agency tend to add a lot of fluff to their resumes and we don't have the resources to check them all. If it's not in the file, it is difficult for us to verify the truth and veracity of what you've been saying."

"I see. So, a fax to my university to confirm my degree would have been too difficult?" I challenge.

"Well, I've recently taken over your case, I can't speak to what my coworkers did or didn't do," he waffles.

"It might be me, but that doesn't sound like too much of an apology," I remark sardonically.

"I'm sorry, Lieutenant Ashford, I don't mean to sound that way; I'm trying to explain the limitations of our agency."

"For argument's sake, let's say I accept your non-apology apology. What does that mean for my case?"

"Well, when someone has the kind of work history you've demonstrated paired with your education, the employment options open up greatly."

"So, you're saying before I was only some poor blind schmuck, you had to help?"

"No sir, that's not what I'm saying at all. We didn't have the whole picture. We try to give top-notch service to all of our clients, regardless of their education level."

"You'll pardon me if I disagree. When I tried to

present you with evidence supporting my work history, you accused me of fabricating my qualifications. That's not exactly top-notch service."

"I repeat, if it's not in the file, there's not a lot we can do," Holmes asserts.

"This 'missing documentation' as you call it mysteriously arrived in my file after almost a year?" I ask skeptically.

"Lieutenant Ashford, I don't know what to tell you. Our picture of your employment history has suddenly become much clearer, and I would like to reevaluate your occupational plan."

"Okay, so tell me, I've spent most of my life as an adult either pursuing flight school, completing flight school, or being a pilot. Exactly how does that translate into great career opportunities for a guy who can't see?"

"That kind of defeatist attitude won't get you far in the job market, Lieutenant Ashford," he scolds.

I scrub my hand down my face and take a deep breath as I try to keep a lid on my temper. I hate it when people are condescending. It's like an emotional minefield.

"Look, I don't know what world you live in. But in the world I live in, I'm blind. People treat me differently because of it. It's not defeatist to recognize that. It's called being realistic. You all sent me to a sweatshop phone bank to work. I did that for too many months to count. The only reason I'm still not doing it is because the supervisor was a jerk and wouldn't let me take time off when my sister got shot."

"That's unfortunate," Mr. Holmes interjects. "We always hope our placement locations are compassionate and understanding."

"Well, this one was not. The argument over my sister was only the tip of the iceberg. Yet, I was the second highest performing employee. I kept my head down, and I worked hard even though the job didn't play to any of my strengths and was — except for a few bright spots — basically pure crap."

"You should've said something. We would've tried to find you alternative employment."

"Did you actually read my file?" I huff, my patience near the breaking point.

"Yes, I told you I recently reviewed your file," he answers.

"Did anybody work on my file before you got to it?" I let out a frustrated breath.

"Umm… honestly … your case didn't exactly get the level of attention we would like to see from our agency. For that, I deeply apologize."

I slump back in my chair. "I guess I should be relieved, because I wondered if I was talking to a wall when I would call this place to let them know what was going on. You're telling me I basically got empty lip-service?"

"Well, I probably shouldn't say more. But your case was not handled ideally."

"And now something has changed and I will suddenly get better service?" I ask, unable to keep the sarcasm out of my voice.

"That is our goal, Lieutenant Ashford."

"Well, if nothing else, this should be interesting."

Tayanita comes up behind me and rubs my neck. "You seem tense. Is this about the barbecue this afternoon?" she asks softly. "I promise, Ketki and I won't abandon you in a strange place. Besides, all of Mark and Shelby's friends are very nice. I don't think you'll have a problem getting along with them."

I set my headphones on the desk as I respond, "No, it's not that. I had a weird meeting with the employment agency the other day. Now they are sending me job announcements from all over the map."

"You mean from out of state?"

"No, not exactly, although some of them are. They cover anything and everything. One is for a manager of a 7-Eleven, and the other is for a college professor. I don't know that I'm qualified for either of those positions. It's difficult to sort through these with my screen reader."

"Okay, after we get back from the barbecue, I'll help you look through them and see if I can find anything interesting."

"You know I hate relying on you for this stuff. Not being able to handle it on my own is frustrating."

"John, don't worry about it. I help my siblings look for work too and they have no visual impairments. Looking for work is challenging for everyone."

I heave out a deep sigh. "It's days like this I miss the Coast Guard. I loved having steady, stable work. I feel so useless."

"I know it's frustrating, but something will come along that's perfect for you. I'm sure of it."

"John, I thought you would never get here. You won't believe what I was able to program into my game. I have been working on it for weeks and weeks," Ketki exclaims as soon as we arrive on her doorstep.

I grimace. "Ketki, I'm sorry, but I don't do much gaming these days. It's hard for screen-readers to decipher graphics."

"I know! That's why what I'm working on with Tristan is so cool. I want you to test it out. When I try it, it's hard for me to know how it works because I helped make the game and so I know where things are."

"You design video games?" I ask, trying to disguise my surprise.

"Yeah. Where have you been? I thought you heard *Etsi* and me discuss it the other day."

"I probably did, but as soon as you guys started chatting about gaming, I tuned out," I admit. "I'm sorry. It's a force of habit. I figured the conversation didn't have much to do with me."

"Well, what I'm trying to tell you is I worked with Tristan to make the game more accessible to you."

"Wow! I'm impressed you would even think about that. What game is this?"

"I'm not allowed to tell you. I have a nondisclosure agreement with Tristan. I can show you the end product. We've been working on it forever. Tristan had to change it up because of some security flaws, but he thinks we have it all fixed now."

"If it's that secret, maybe you shouldn't show me."

"No, that's the cool thing, Tristan will be here soon, and he told me as long as you understood the game isn't market-ready yet, I could allow you to play."

"Ketki, why don't you let John catch his breath! After Tristan gets here, John can sign a nondisclosure agreement too, if that's what's required."

The frustration is clear in Ketki's voice as she responds, "Okay. Fine. But it's not fair. I have been working on this for months. I wanted to surprise John."

"I know. But it's better for Tristan's trial if he does everything by the book. You know that. You've been working with him for several years."

Ketki sighs in a manner that almost sounds like a growl. "*Arghh!* I hate it when you're all logical and make sense. I like life more when I don't have to follow the rules. I hope it doesn't take Tristan forever to get here."

"I'm sorry, kiddo. I'm sure it will be great whenever you can show me. Do you want to introduce me around?"

Ketki still sounds annoyed. "Okay … It's not like I'm doing anything better right now. You've already met my dad. Do you need to meet him again?"

"Since I'm a guest in your home, it might be nice for me to stop by and say hello," I answer with a shrug.

"Did Tayanita tell you this is a family barbecue?" Ketki asks as she takes my hand. "We have them all the time. It's not like you have to have your company manners on here."

"Well, that might be so. But I want to be polite. If I weren't, my mom would give me a stern lecture."

"How would your mom find out?" Ketki asks quizzically.

"I don't know for sure. Moms always seem to be able to figure everything out."

"You're telling me, I'm about to have two of them. I can't get away with anything."

"I guess those are the breaks. But look on the bright side, you've got two people who care about you a lot. That's better than some people have."

"Geez, have you been taking lessons from my dad? He talks that way sometimes too."

"No, I think that's what you get when you gain some perspective," I answer. "It's scary how closely I echo the advice of my parents. I'm not sure when I turned into them, but I guess it's not necessarily a bad thing."

Ketki carefully weaves me through the backyard until she stops in front of someone. "Dad, remember John? *Etsi* brought her boyfriend. I'm showing him around until Tristan comes and then we're going to play video games."

"Ki, did you even bother to ask John if he wants to play?" Mark gently chastises.

"I did, but Tayanita said I had to wait until Tristan came. Sometimes, it's a pain to have so many grown-ups in my life."

Mark touches my wrist. "Thanks for coming today. Nita looks happy. Probably the best I've seen her. I hear you're responsible for that."

"I can't take all the credit, she makes me happy too."

"I understand you played chess with Ketki. So, I don't need to warn you about how competitive she is," Mark advises.

"I am aware, although, Ketki has grounds to be proud. She is currently holding onto our trophy until I can beat her again. She's won nine weeks in a row. I don't believe I've ever had such a worthy opponent."

"I appreciate you are one of the few who are brave enough to still play. Most people, including me, have given up playing against her. She left me in the dust a long time ago."

Another voice enters the conversation. She is not wearing Tayanita's perfume so I'm assuming it might be Shelby.

"Are you guys talking about chess again?"

"Yeah, Ketki is killing John over here. So far he has been gracious in defeat."

The woman laughs. "I probably shouldn't be spilling strategic information, but it's nice for her to play against such a skilled player. You've got her going to the library to look up advanced moves. It's been a while since she's had any real competition."

"Don't talk about me like I'm not here, Mom. John already knows how good I am because he's been playing against me for a few months."

"Don't gloat, Ketki," Shelby cautions.

"It's not gloating if I'm telling the truth, is it?"

"The line is close. I can tell you this honestly since I used to skate on that line all the time," I warn.

"What do you mean?"

"When I was a new pilot, I used to brag to all my friends about how good I was. It wasn't too long before I had a lot fewer friends. They got sick of hearing me talk about myself."

"Bummer," Ketki says. "I try not to be a jerk, though."

"I'm sure you're not. I was telling you what I used to do when I was younger. I was kind of full of myself back in the day."

"Weird. You're a nice man now," Ketki comments succinctly.

"I think he's a nice guy too," Tayanita says as she slides up next to me.

"John, I'd like you to meet my friends Jessica and Mitch," she says as she helps direct my attention to my left.

"It's nice to meet you, John," Jessica greets. "I can't tell you how happy I am to see you here. Tayanita has been alone for way too long."

Someone clears their throat. "Jess, we've just met the man. Can you wait a bit until you throw them an engagement party?"

"I'm sorry. Mitch is right. I don't always think before I talk."

"It's all right. It's perfectly normal to want your friend to be happy," I reply. I grin and reach my hand out for her to shake.

"Mitch says I treat marriage like a contagious virus. I want everyone to catch it, even if it's against their will," Jessica says with a laugh.

"You sound like my mom. She and Dad are like marriage evangelists. She plays matchmaker with people in line at the grocery store," I comment.

"Does your family like Nita? Do they think she is as awesome as the rest of us do?"

"Jess! Stop embarrassing the man," Mitch warns with a snort of laughter. "Sorry, John. Once she's on a roll, nothing much dissuades her."

"It's fine," I respond with a smile. "My family does like Tayanita a lot. She became a bit of a hero when she helped translate medical jargon after my sister was hurt."

"Yeah, Nita is smart like that."

"Hey, do you mind if I change the subject? Not that I'm uncomfortable or anything; I would like to talk dogs with you."

"Search and Rescue, protection, or service?" Mitch asks.

"I guess a Seeing Eye dog would be considered a service dog," I answer. "It is becoming clear this blindness thing is permanent. I'd like to know if you train dogs for people like me."

"I do," Mitch confirms. "It will be several months before we have another graduating class of dogs, though."

"I expected that. I've heard there are waiting lists several years long."

"That is definitely true about some of the better-known programs, but Hope's Haven is new enough to the service dog industry that there isn't much of a waiting list yet."

His announcement takes my breath away. One of the reasons I haven't pursued the idea of a guide dog is because I'm afraid it will just lead to disappointment.

Grabbing Blue's hand for support, I ask, "So, if I'd like to get on that waiting list, what do I need to do?"

"Come see us at Hope's Haven and we'll get the process started."

# CHAPTER NINETEEN

# TAYANITA

"John looks like he fits in great. Padre-pop hasn't stopped talking to him for about the last forty-five minutes," Ivy comments as I go into the kitchen to grab a drink.

"Yeah, I noticed. They're probably comparing all the hotspots they've been to. John misses being in the service. Talking with Isaac is probably like talking to all of his crew mates."

"Still, my dad rarely opens up that much." Ivy peeks through the bar area to watch them interact. "Your guy is good. He didn't even flinch when Marcus pulled out his protective big brother routine."

"I felt bad when Marcus started asking him about his job," I admit. "He went a little too far, considering he's not even my brother."

Ivy shrugs. "Well, you can't say Marcus is acting inconsistently. He does that with virtually everyone. Once you've been adopted by the Ink'd Deep crew, you're in for life. It's like the Mafia or something."

"I think John is getting a feel for that. I prepared him for questions from Shelby, but I didn't realize all the rest of you would be quite so curious about us. I travel on the perimeter of your circle."

"Are you kidding? You're Ki's mom. That puts you smack in the middle of the group. Have you not been on several shopping trips with us?"

"Well … yes. I go with Shelby and Ketki," I explain.

"I hate to tell you this, but those are our bonding trips. If you weren't part of our crew, you wouldn't be there," Ivy counters.

"Silly me. I thought we were just buying clothes."

"Don't worry about it. Our unusual hazing methods tend to go unnoticed."

"Just so you know, I hate the dress you guys convinced me to get," I respond as their methods become clear.

Ivy giggles. "Yeah, we knew that, but you handled it with such grace. That's why we knew you were one of us."

"That's underhanded," I smirk. "I guess I can donate it to a charity now without the fear of hurting anyone's feelings."

"Oh my Gosh! You mean to tell me you kept that thing?" she exclaims. "You are a dedicated friend."

Ketki dashes into the kitchen and pulls on my arm. "*Etsi*, what's taking you so long? Tristan is finally here. We can start playing. We're waiting for you."

"Okay, okay I'm coming. I just stopped to talk to Ivy." I grab my drink and walk into the living room. Ketki runs to her seat.

John is sitting on the couch between Tristan and Ketki. He is holding a video game controller with a dubious look on his face.

"Ketki, are you as good at video games as you are at chess?" John asks with some trepidation.

"I'm not supposed to brag, but I'm better at video games, especially this one because I helped program it."

"Did you fix the glitch that was causing screen flicker?" Marcus asks.

"I think so. Everyone's screen resolution is different. So it's a little tricky."

"I have played nothing more difficult than solitaire since my accident. I don't know how effective I'll be. I know for sure I won't beat you," John cautions as he handles the controller like it's a foreign object.

After a moment, he looks at Ketki with total astonishment as he says, "Did you braille this for me?"

Ketki looks smug. "Of course I did. It'll help you play better, right?"

"Probably. Like I said, I haven't done this in a long time. I'm not familiar with your specific game, so it'll be even more difficult for me."

"Take a deep breath, Ashford," Isaac instructs. "If I know Ketki at all, she's got you covered."

"You know it. I've been working on this for months," Ketki confirms.

"Okay, I guess I am a willing guinea pig," John says.

"The way this game is set up is the menu is across the top at noon and your tools are down at the bottom at six."

"How will I know where my player is?"

"*Etsi*, can you please make sure the volume is turned

up?" Ketki asks.

Knowing my daughter as well as I do, I think she told me that to make John comfortable. She always goes through her video game settings before she starts a game. Nevertheless, I walk over to the gaming console and check the settings on the monitor.

"This takes a minute to start because I didn't want to interrupt Declan's music at the start of the game. So, wait a moment until the music is through."

"Roger," John responds.

"Okay," Ketki interrupts as the music fades away. "The movements are the same as they are with most other games. Press your A button if you want to pick something up."

"Umm, Ki — I can't see anything on the screen, remember? How am I going to know what the rest of the players see?"

"In three, two, one," Ketki mumbles under her breath. "Okay, move your joystick on side B."

A computerized voice announces, "You are standing in the middle of the screen. One click in either direction will move you five degrees. Would you like to customize your character? To vote yes, click A. To vote no, click B."

"Ketki, did you add enhanced narration to your game so I could play?" John asks in a shocked whisper.

"I did. It was hard to play the game blindfolded, but I did for a couple of weeks so I could tell what needed to be described."

Tears roll down my face as I realize how much empathy Ketki has for John's limitations. That must've taken hours and hours of programming time.

John's voice breaks as he reaches around Ketki shoulders and pulls her in close for a hug. "Thank you. This is probably the nicest thing anyone has done for me. I can't tell you how much it means to me."

Ketki looks around the room with a puzzled expression as she asks, "Why is everyone crying? I made it so John could play video games. Everybody should be able to play video games because they're fun."

"They haven't been much fun for me recently, but I think this might change all that. I don't even know what to say other than thank you from the bottom of my heart."

Tristan clears his throat. "Ketki's idea to make this accessible for you raised a whole level of concern for me as a programmer. I had never looked at the overall accessibility of my games for people with disabilities. I decided I want to make it a project."

"I thought you were a security specialist. I thought Identity Bank was all about tracking down Internet fraud and missing people," John blurts. "I had no idea you were a video game developer."

"Well, Isaac and I have our fingers in a lot of different pies. We do some law enforcement stuff, military subcontracting, Internet safety programs, and obviously, I still do the games."

"That's a lot of different specialties to coordinate," John comments.

"I know. We are looking to branch out. I was wondering if you might be interested in joining our team."

"It depends on your answers to my questions. Am I actually going to have a real job or am I going to be a poster-person so you get tax credits?" John challenges.

"Isaac can tell you I don't make hiring decisions lightly. If I'm inviting you to join our team, you will work your butt off," Tristan says solemnly.

"In that case, tell me where to apply," John answers with a slow smile.

"Not yet!" Ketki exclaims. "You came over to have fun at the barbecue, so we need to play video games. I want to know if someone who doesn't know the game as good as I do can navigate through it."

"Have no fear, Ketki. You worked super hard to make this game playable for me. So, I plan to play it until my thumbs fall off," John replies as he scoots forward on the couch and grabs the controller.

Ketki looks up at me with a grin. "You made a good choice, *Etsi*. It's hard to find someone who likes video games as much as we do."

"I agree. For lots of reasons, I think I made a perfect choice."

The atmosphere in the car on the way home is strange. It's almost as if there is too much emotion to fit in such a small space.

"What did you think of my friends?" I venture carefully.

"I'm not surprised they're chill. After hearing Ketki describe Jade's hair, piercings and tattoos, I am a tad disappointed I can't see her. The impact must be intense."

"It's funny, I've been friends with her long enough I don't even notice that stuff anymore. Ketki has always been totally enamored with all things Jade."

"So, you expect her to come home one day with matching tattoos?" John teases.

"I made Jade, Rogue and Marcus all promise they wouldn't touch Ketki until she's well into adulthood. I'm thinking forty might work."

"That kid of yours is something else. I can't believe she did all that so I could play video games with her."

"I agree. It's stunning, but Ketki has been into video games for as long as anyone can remember. That's how we met. I was playing with her in an online role-playing game before I realized she was my daughter."

"Wow! That must have been a strange shock," I remark. "It's more than technical skills, though. It's the fact she thought of it on her own. Your daughter is exceptional."

"I'm not arguing. However, you don't get to give me any credit."

"Why not? As nearly as I can tell, you've been involved in her life since you reunited. Apparently, you were part of her life beforehand as well. She obviously looks to you as a mentor. Video games aside, she thinks you are one of the coolest people she's ever met."

"How do you know this?" I ask.

"Ketki and I spend a great deal of time playing chess and doing homework. You know your daughter well enough to know she's rarely quiet about anything. When she has an opinion, she is more than happy to share it. We talk about lots of things, you included."

"I guess I haven't given a lot of thought to how Ketki views me," I admit.

"For some reason, I don't quite believe you because you think about everything. It's one of the things I totally love about you. You examine every problem from every angle. You'll forgive me if I think you might be fibbing," John answers with an amused grin.

"Okay, I guess I'm busted. I think about Ketki all the time. For a long time, I was afraid to get involved with her because I wasn't sure how much grace Mark was going to allow me for all my past screw ups."

"By all appearances, you all seem to have succeeded in blending your families. I don't think you need to hold your distance anymore. Ketki is obviously attached to you and wants you in her life. I don't see that changing anytime soon," John says.

"I'm trying to be optimistic, but honestly, I'm a little afraid that once Shelby and Mark tie the knot, it might be easier to exclude me from Ketki's life. Before you and I met, I think I convinced myself I deserved it. But, that's not what I want anymore."

"Have you told Mark and Shelby this?" John asks.

"I've talked it over with Shelby a bit."

"Did she seem opposed to you staying in Ketki's life? I mean, I know I met her today, but you guys sound like you're good friends. I didn't pick up any vibes from her that she at all resents your presence in Ketki's life. In fact, we were talking about her career day and she seems to credit you for single-handedly making it a hit."

I sigh. "You're right. It's probably a silly and unfounded fear on my part. Shelby specifically said they won't force me out of Ketki's life. I guess I'm afraid everything is too good to be true."

"I can't tell you I don't often feel the same way. But,

maybe you and I should focus on moving forward and being a little less afraid of the past."

"So, you don't think there is such a thing as being too happy?" I press.

"I guess it depends on the situation, but from where I stand, I think things are going about as well as they possibly can. I don't know about you, but I have never been this much in love."

"There was a time in my life I thought I was in love with Mark, but I know now I wasn't. It took meeting you for me to learn the true meaning of love."

As I pull the car into the driveway, John reaches out and grabs my hand. He brings it up to his lips and kisses my knuckles. "As much as I like your friends, I've been waiting for us to be alone all day. I'm a rather hands-on, concrete kinda guy and I want to do more than tell you I love you."

"It's been a long day, but I could so get on board with the plan." I squeeze his hand.

I walk around the car and wait for him to exit. He holds onto my elbow as we walk toward the front door. As soon as we cross the threshold, he sets down his white cane and grabs me around the waist. "Okay, we're in my territory. I've got you now."

"You sure do in more ways than you could ever know," I whisper as we head toward the bedroom.

I kick off my shoes and climb into the middle of the bed.

John takes off his clothes in an unintentionally sexy striptease.

As a nurse, I have seen all sorts of bodies. Generally,

I pay next to no notice, but it's different with John. I find his physique to be endlessly fascinating. His abs are like a work of art.

He crawls in bed with me and kisses my shoulder. "Mmm… you smell like coconuts and pineapple." He moves up and kisses the spot under my ear. "In this spot, you smell like vanilla."

"The piña colada smell is compliments of some organic sunscreen Jade wanted me to try. I couldn't tell you if it actually works well as regular sunscreen, but it smells yummy."

"I approve," John says before he captures my lips in a hot, searing kiss. He reaches up and plunges his fingers through my hair. "Have I told you recently about how crazy I am over your hair?"

"Not today. But, I am aware of your devotion," I tease as John runs his fingers down the full length of my hair.

"Well, I do. I adore it and everything else about you."

As John tenderly runs his thumbs down the side of my face, I turn my face and kiss the pad of his thumb.

"I think I've had enough words for today. Show me how much you love me."

John pulls me close and whispers, "I thought you'd never ask."

# CHAPTER TWENTY

# JOHN

I CAN TELL BY the way the sound echoes hollowly off the walls that the headquarters of Identity Bank borders on the gargantuan.

"Thanks for coming in today, John. Can I show you around?"

I never know how to answer that question. It's not like he can literally show me around because that would be pointless. I shrug. "Sure, I'm interested in what you've got going here."

"I don't know how much of my story you know. I started Identity Bank when I was still a teenager. In those days, I was an insatiably curious kid with a knack for computers," Tristan explains, carrying on the conversation as we walk forward. From the way he's moving, I guess he has served as a guide before.

"What you're telling me is that you were a lot like Ketki?" I quip.

"Scarily so. Putting her on my testing team was the smartest thing I ever did."

"How did you get involved with the gaming industry?"

"Again, it was my curiosity and boredom getting the best of me. I figured out a way to better protect phone apps from viruses. That gave me enough capital to pursue the fun stuff. It turned out I was good at creating games and a little ahead of the curve."

"So, why don't you do the gaming stuff full-time? It seems like that might be more lucrative."

"It might've been, but Identity Bank has always been my baby, and I've got personal reasons for wanting to help people solve their cyber mysteries and find long-lost family members."

"At the party, you said you do a variety of stuff with the military. Where does that fall?"

"That was a side of my career which developed accidentally. I became known as an expert in preventing identity theft and cyber loss. Soon, I was being called as an expert witness in fraud cases which put me in touch with a lot of law enforcement folks. I testified in three cases involving NCIS and their attorneys, which was the break I needed to get my foot in the door with the military."

"Talk about being in the right place at the right time."

"You don't have to tell me. I've been incredibly lucky. I even met my wife while I was working a case."

"I guess I don't have the only story of finding the woman I love on the job."

"No, that's not unique to you. Rosa and Isaac met that way as did Jade and Declan, and Jessica and Mitch, to name a few."

"Isaac told me he works with you as well. What does he do?"

"Even though he's my father-in-law, parts of his past are a secret. But he used to work with one of the clandestine agencies tracking down art theft and other valuables. His department was absorbed into another one, and he elected to retire and come work for me. We work on a lot of cases together, but we also run Elliott's House in several locations."

"Elliott's House? I'm not familiar with it. I'm sorry."

"They are support programs for kids who have lost their parents. We have a few camps and some residential programs going on. But basically, it's a place where kids can feel free to talk about their pain and grief without being judged."

"I get the feeling Elliott's House is where your personal connection comes in?"

"Your instincts are right on. The centers are named after my little brother. He lost his mother when he was a child."

"Come again?" I ask trying to follow the story.

"When my mom was a teenager, she gave up a child for adoption. I started Identity Bank so I could help my mom find her daughter."

"You mean your sister?" I clarify.

"Technically she was. Since I never got to know her, Francine didn't seem real to me. Locating her was simply a puzzle I needed to solve. Still, finding her meant the world to my mother. She passed away from a dental procedure and my mom ended up raising her son, Elliott."

"You're not kidding that all this is personal to you."

"No I'm not. It's all impossibly intertwined. So, that

was a long answer for why I don't just do software and video game design."

"How do you keep all of those operations straight?"

"It's a lot easier now that I'm not working out of my parents' basement or my college dorm room. In this building, the operations of Identity Bank are confined to the first floor, we do software development on the second and Elliott's House and any other charitable stuff we do is located on the third floor." Tristan stops abruptly and says, "There is a conference table right in front of you if you want to have a seat."

"Thanks." I pull out the chair and sit down. "It sounds like you have a diverse organization here. I'm not exactly sure how you're going to work me into it," I admit with a shrug.

"Well, when I was clearing up the other matter for you, I was reading your background and realized you have many skills that'll work well within our organization."

"What do you mean other matter?" I ask skeptically.

"Didn't you get a read in on the final report?" Tristan counters with surprise in his voice.

"No, I don't think so," I reply sharply.

"This is why I need someone with your management skills here. Since our manager's husband was stationed in Turkey, our whole chain of command has been thrown off."

"Tristan, I don't know if it's my limitations or if I have been hit over the head with the stupid stick, but I have no earthly idea what you're talking about."

"Oh, that's a problem. I'll be right back. I need to go grab a file."

I hear his chair roll backward and the door close behind him.

All this cloak and dagger stuff reminds me of the investigation into the incident which caused my blindness. I feel a shiver go up my spine.

In no time at all, Tristan reenters the room. I hear a file slap down on the table.

"What's going on here?" I ask as I fidget in my chair.

Tristan shuffles what seems like reams of paper. "I'll be able to tell you in a second."

It's so awkward to sit here like a bump on the log trying to figure out what's going on around me.

"Okay, the client gave us permission to share the information with you."

"Who is your client?" I demand. "I know I didn't hire you."

"Well … umm…" Tristan stammers as he flips through more pages.

"Wait, don't even bother to tell me. I think I have this figured out. I thought Tayanita trusted me. I guess I was wrong. She probably hired you to research my background to see if I'm some pervy criminal or something."

"I think you're jumping to all the wrong conclusions. Besides, Tayanita isn't even the client."

"Oh great! That means it's probably Mark or Shelby trying to find reasons to exclude Tayanita from Ketki's life. That's even worse in my book."

"John, stop and listen to me," Tristan commands in a level voice.

"Start talking. You have a lot to explain. I have done nothing to warrant a clandestine background search."

Things are silent for a moment while Tristan shuffles through more papers. The sound of my rapid breathing is deafening. For every second that passes, I'm getting more steamed at the situation.

"You gotta be kidding me!" Tristan says with disgust.

"What?" I ask. "Macklin, you are freaking me out big time. Just get to it, will you?"

"Sorry, I'm frustrated with my staff right now. This case should have been completely briefed by now and the information shared with you, I apologize."

"It's funny, a lot of people in charge of my future have been telling me they're sorry for whatever they do or don't do. It's getting a little old," I grumble.

"I can understand why you're frustrated. I would be too. In fact, I would be completely pissed off if I found out someone was looking into my past without my knowledge. That's not what we try to do here at Identity Bank."

"Then tell me what the heck happened."

"Your file came into our office the day Ivy had an art show out of town. I was not even here. Otherwise, it would've been routed to me."

"Stop giving excuses and spit it out, will you?"

"Going back to reconstruct the file, it seems Mark wanted to talk to me directly about your case, but I wasn't here, so our new employee, Kalinda did the intake for me."

"So?" I probe.

"With the staffing changes, the file didn't get flagged

appropriately, and I never got the updates about your case. I assumed you knew all about it."

"There should've never been a case!" I respond angrily. "I don't understand what the heck you're talking about."

"It was nothing sinister, it was merely a breakdown in communication. It seems like Tayanita asked Mark if he could do anything about your employment situation. She was concerned you had been treated unfairly and wanted to know if there was anything Mark, as an attorney, could do."

"Blue had no right to tell Mark anything. I don't want him thinking I am a freakin' weakling. I can handle my own affairs," I insist.

"I'm sure you can, which is why you're here today. I'd like to give you a job."

"Wait… if Tayanita called in Mark, how did you get involved?"

"Mark was going to send the agency a routine, generic threatening letter with a copy of a cease and desist order. However, the more he dug, the nastier things got. He figured he needed some outside help to figure it out."

"That doesn't explain a lot," I grouse.

"At that point, Identity Bank got involved. We were able to do a much deeper search into your background than Mark could."

"Is this supposed to be making me feel better? I have to tell you — you're pissing me off."

"Before you rip my head off, you might want to hear what we found."

"I hope it's worthy of all the nightmarish scenarios flying through my brain at this point."

"Put quite simply, the occupational and educational path the placement agency provided for you was drastically inappropriate. Consequently, I set out to figure out why. It didn't take me long to confirm you are a great student and that you graduated at the top of your class. Your work history, paid and not paid is exceptionally varied and you are technically savvy."

"I think I told you guys a little about my background on the first day we met. Job hunting is not a clean, pristine sport, even under the best circumstances. My situation is far less than ideal when it comes to finding a job. I am not exactly qualified to do what I was trained to do anymore. Even the so-called 'experts' are having trouble placing me."

"That's where we come in. When things didn't add up, Mark became suspicious and called Identity Bank. It took us a while to puzzle through what was happening, but Isaac called a few of his contacts within the military, and we got it straightened out."

"Got what straightened out? I'm frustrated because none of this is making any sense."

"We determined you were getting poor service from the Veterans Administration because someone purposefully fed them wrong information."

"WTF! Why would somebody do that? I was in the hospital fighting for my life when I left the Coast Guard. It wasn't like it was a voluntary decision," I explain angrily.

"John, I don't think anybody is suggesting you did. However, this appears to have something to do with the accident and resulting investigation."

"How is that possible? I wasn't responsible for the investigation or the resulting findings. I left the Coast Guard a long time ago."

"Apparently, the trainee you were working with came from a well-heeled family. They were not happy you were not held responsible for the accident. So, they took it upon themselves to make sure you paid some sort of price."

"Price? What do you mean?"

"Well, someone was well enough connected that they were able to persuade somebody to doctor your military records to look like you have substantially less experience and aptitude."

"I don't understand how they could even do that!" I exclaimed. "I was a freaking pilot. Did they think I got my certifications from a Cracker Jack box?"

"The details are still fuzzy. It's clear someone tampered with your personnel records. All indications are it was revenge for the outcome of the investigation into your accident."

"Is it possible things could move from the filing cabinet to real life?"

"Meaning?" Tristan asks warily.

"I don't know if anyone had a chance to tell you, but I was nearly run down by a hit-and-run motorist a while back."

Tristan squirms around in his chair but does not get up as he says, "I guess it's entirely possible. However, I don't have enough information at this moment to tell you definitively one way or another."

After a few moments, I lean forward in my seat and put my elbows on the conference table as I say, "You need to give me time to process today. I don't even know where to start. I can't believe Tayanita would even instigate this type of thing without talking to me first and why would she involve her ex?"

"I can't speak to your communication style as a couple or the reasons she didn't tell you she was trying to figure out what was going on. I can say you don't need to worry about Tayanita's relationship with Mark. The only relationship they have is as former friends and co-parents to Ketki. Mark is so far gone over Shelby, it's not funny."

"I appreciate your honesty today. I've got so many layers of this to unpack, it'll take a while for me to wrap my brain around it all. I think I'd like to wait to talk about any job opportunities with you. I need to settle down and think this through. Honestly, I am still stunned."

"I get it. People often have conflicting responses to how they feel about the information we unearth. I'm all right with that. Let me know when you're ready to talk shop again. I would love to have you as an employee. This project with Ketki is important to me."

"I'll let you know what I sort out," I promise as I gather up my things to go.

It is safe to say this day went nothing like I expected it to. Now what?

# CHAPTER TWENTY-ONE

# TAYANITA

TODAY HAS BEEN AWFUL in every sense of the word. First, a patient who had undergone an epidural threw up on my favorite pair of shoes and later in the day, we lost a patient on the table.

I understand it's one of the risks of my job. However, it never gets any easier. My arms are still sore from assisting with CPR. To add insult to injury, one of the other nurses accidentally kicked me in the jaw when we were trading positions.

Fortunately, I was not the person who had the duty to tell Mr. Kester his wife would not be coming home. Sometimes even with all the advances in medicine, we cannot undo the damage from a massive stroke. Even though I know we did all we could do; it still makes me profoundly sad.

I am more than a little ready to be home and righteously spoiled. It's one perk of being in a relationship. John is always attentive to my physical and emotional needs and tonight, I'll be taking him up on that care. I need some industrial-strength cuddles to get over my hellacious day.

As I let myself into our home, it is unusually quiet. Usually, John is listening to some sports event on the radio or has a news story running in the background. However, there is no sound in the whole house and it doesn't smell like anything has been cooked recently.

John is supposed to be here. Instinctively, my heart rate kicks up as I start to search for him. I try, with little success, to put on my professional demeanor and approach the situation with a sense of calm.

The sound of my own pounding heart echoes in my ears as I frantically search room to room. I about faint from relief when I find him in the back bedroom I use as a den hunched over his laptop with headphones on.

I walk over and rub his shoulders. He jumps and flinches. "You had me worried."

"Why? Don't you trust me to take care of myself?" John snaps as he pulls away from me.

The bitterness in his voice catches me off guard.

"Of course I do," I protest. "My medical training kicks in sometimes and I'm a bit overprotective."

"So, that's what we're calling it these days?" he snarls sarcastically.

"I don't understand; all I said was I was scared when I couldn't find you."

"Last I checked, you are not my mother and don't have a right to keep tabs on every single thing I do in my life," John responds.

"Okay … I'm sorry … I guess. Although, I don't understand why you're upset. Things were not the way they usually are when I came home. That's all I was saying."

"I don't know. It seems like you want to keep much closer tabs on me than that."

"John, I've had a long day. Can you tell me what we're talking about? I have no idea."

"I went to go see Tristan today."

"Yeah, I figured you would. He offered you a job. I don't understand the problem."

"I find that hard to believe since you've been spreading my problems all over town. Is there anyone who doesn't know? I bet you Mark got a good laugh about the fact I can't even support myself these days."

"Mark wouldn't do that!" I exclaim. "He's not that kind of guy; he has never been."

"See, I figured you were probably still in love with the dude, because why else would you hang around him all the time?"

"I am not in love with Mark," I whisper in a broken voice.

"Funny, you could've fooled me. It seems the two of you probably had a field day talking about all my problems," John accuses.

"That's why you're mad at me? Because I tried to get you help —"

"Did I tell you I need any help? I'm good at asking people if I need them to do something for me. I don't recall giving you permission to discuss me with your ex," John spits.

This on top of my horrible day from hell is too much.

I spin John's office chair around so he's facing me.

"Look. That's enough," I assert, letting my temper show. "You're right. I didn't have your express permission to go talk to Mark. I should have asked. Honestly, I didn't think it'd be any big deal. You and I help each other all the time. We have been through some serious crap."

"Exactly! But that crap is our business, no one else's," John argues.

"I didn't mean to upset you. Mark is one of the sharpest legal minds I know."

"Yeah, yeah I know Mark is perfect, Shelby is amazing, and I'm a couch potato who sits around watching TV all day."

"Mark isn't perfect. If he was perfect, we'd probably be together. But he's found somebody else, and you know what? I'm totally okay with that because I don't love him. I love you. I thought you knew," I reply.

"Then why are you even talking to him? This doesn't have to do with Ketki. You didn't have to talk to them about Ketki, unless you don't trust me to be with her."

"Oh my Gosh! Obviously, I don't feel that way because I introduced you to her. What is your problem?"

"I'll tell you what my problem is. I went to a job interview today expecting to get a great new job. But, instead, I found out Tristan had gone deep-sea diving into my background. Why?"

I sit back in the chair, astonished by this new turn of events.

"I honestly don't know why Tristan is involved. I went to go see Mark because you were being discriminated against by both your employer and the agency which was supposed to be helping you find a job. I wanted to see if there was anything we could do. I know when Mark writes a letter, people tend to sit up and take notice. I wanted you to be treated better than you were."

"You don't get it, do you? The last person I want to know I'm struggling is your ex-husband. I can't measure up to being your first love. So, I definitely didn't want you to go host a pity party on my behalf," John argues. "I bet he was real impressed by the fact I can't get a job."

"You have no idea how much I wish you'd been in that meeting with me. Because if you had, you would've known the only reason I was there was because I was pissed off people were screwing you over."

John shakes his head and rolls his eyes at me as he says, "Whatever!"

"No! *Not whatever.* You're right. I should not have gone to talk to him without you present. Not because there's anything weird between us, but because you're right, it's private stuff. Do you know what we spent most of the time talking about?"

"I couldn't venture a guess," John responds cynically. "I wasn't there, remember?"

"We talked about how much he loves Shelby and can't wait to be married to her."

"I bet that stung a little. Now you're stuck with me."

"Knock it off, John. I don't know how to get you to understand everyone in my circle helps each other. I suspect that's why Mark called Tristan. Believe me, I wasn't part of the decision."

"I understand. Tristan explained to me he sometimes works as a consultant for Hunter's Crossing."

"You know more than I do." I stand up and pace the room. "Tristan must've thought there was some merit to Mark's request, or he wouldn't have taken the case. He's a stickler like that."

"Yeah. That's the other messed up thing."

His words hit me like cold water. "I'm sorry you think our relationship is some messed up thing. I don't happen to agree."

"Look, I didn't say that. I'm pissed at you, that's true. But right now, I've got bigger issues, at least according to Tristan."

"The word is, if Tristan says you've got a problem, you have a problem. So, what's going on?" I ask, unable to keep the concern out of my voice even though my adrenaline is cranking on high. This is the angriest I've ever seen John. This is not how I intended for things to unfold. I wanted Mark to write a simple letter. I'm not sure how this ballooned completely out of control.

John sighs heavily and rakes his hand through his hair.

"It appears besides an aneurysm diagnosis and complete blindness, the fallout from the accident continues."

"What does an incident from training have to do with your life now?" I ask, trying to follow the conversation.

"Remember the rich dude? Apparently, his family doesn't agree with the findings of the safety commission. They want me to pay for what happened to their son for the rest of my career."

"What do they care? You're a civilian now. You don't have access to their son or anyone else's career at this point."

"One would think. Unfortunately, they felt the need to tamper with my military records and make me look less qualified for positions than I actually am."

"Holy federal crime!" I whistle through my teeth.

"That's what Tristan and Isaac said. I guess they were both instrumental in figuring all this out. Isaac said he's going to talk it over with some of his sources in federal law enforcement to see if charges can be pursued. Tampering with my military records is a serious crime."

"To quote Ketki here, 'Well, duh!' In that case, I'm glad Mark brought in Tristan instead of issuing you a letter. It will be hard for them to discriminate once they're behind bars," I state emphatically.

"I guess if I take the long view, I'm glad Tristan is involved too. But, you should've asked me first. I don't like being the subject of a pity party. If you were having trouble with the fact I was unemployed, you should've said something," John argues.

"It wasn't the fact you don't have a job. You gave up your job to take care of your sister. Did you think I would penalize you for that? I didn't get help for you because I feel sorry for you; I got help for you because you need justice. What's going on is wrong. If this so-called employment company is doing all that against you, they're probably doing it against other people too."

"The scary thing is, it seems the employment agency was doing the appropriate thing based on the documentation they had. However, the bad guys in this case wiped my actual history and substituted another one. That scares the crap out of me. I knew blindness would wipe out my future plans as a pilot, I didn't realize someone had the power to erase my actual past."

"They won't be able to get away with this forever."

"Why not? They have been doing it for at least a couple years now. No one has stopped them yet," John observes.

I sit down on a chair across from him and grab his hands. "They did get away with it … before Tristan and Isaac were on the case. Their days as white-collar criminals are over. Now it's all about baking a cake and celebrating the news."

"I wish it was that easy. You know what I kept thinking about all day? What if my real life is in danger and not just my life on paper? After all, someone did hit me with a car. I was doing exactly what I was supposed to be doing, but they almost took me out. What if the line has been crossed between cyber-menacing and real life menacing?"

"I don't know what to say about that. I'm too scared for you to even imagine the possibility. I guess Tristan and Isaac can figure that out somehow. For now, I'll be happy to watch your back. That is, if you still want me around."

John rubs my arms and massages my tense muscles. "Tayanita, even when I am furious with you, there isn't a moment I don't want you in my life."

# CHAPTER TWENTY-TWO

# JOHN

IT FEELS STRANGE TO be here without Ketki. This pizza joint has become our hangout headquarters. They know us so well; they place an order as soon as we come through the door. However, today I'm on a different mission.

"Mr. Ashford, your friends are here. Would you like me to seat them?" my favorite waitress, Lauretta asks.

"Absolutely, can you get me a pitcher of beer too?"

"Sure thing. I know I probably shouldn't say anything, but your friends are uber-sexy in an older guy kind of way."

I chuckle under my breath. "I'll have to take your word for it."

"Oh geez, I'm so sorry. I shouldn't have said anything. That was rude of me," she blurts in a rush.

"Lauretta, it's fine. I thought what you said was funny. I've never spent a great deal of time evaluating the cuteness of my friends, that's all."

"Gotcha. Okay, I'll be right back with your guests."

Her wording strikes me as odd. Do Ketki and I spend

so much time here playing chess and doing homework, even the employees think of this place as our second home?

"So, this is the spot, huh? Ketki tells me you guys have almost reached local celebrity status because you sit in the same spot every day," Mark says as he pulls up a chair and sits down.

"We're not here every day, but often enough to be considered regulars for sure," I answer.

"I want to thank you for playing chess with Ketki. She has a hard time finding people who are willing to play against her because she is so good."

"I am surprised at how evenly we are matched. I was on the chess team in high school. We eventually went to the state tournament and came in second. Your daughter's skills are nothing to sneeze at."

"You're good for her," Mark announces.

"She's good for me too. She has done a lot to make it easier for me to get around and enjoy life. She could have a future in assistive technology."

Mark and Tristan both say, "That's true."

"I think the issue won't be finding enough things for Ki to do. I think her problem will be narrowing it down to half a dozen," Tristan adds.

"That sounds like somebody else I know, Mr. Macklin," I remark pointedly.

"I know, right? There's not much Tristan can't do," Mark says with a chuckle.

"Have some pizza. I've got beer coming,"

"I never turn down pizza from this place, but to what do we owe the honor?"

"I asked the two of you to meet me here because I want to clear the air about a few things," I state.

"This is about me consulting with Tristan, isn't it?"

"The whole thing is strange. I don't know why my girlfriend told the whole world about my problems, and I don't know why you disseminated the information even further. Aren't you bound by some sort of special rules or something?"

"I didn't get the sense from Tayanita she was gossiping about the two of you. She was genuinely concerned about how you were being treated. Initially, I was planning to write a big, scary letter on my letterhead and see if that would be effective in resolving the problem. It often is."

"So how did this thing grow from a letter?"

"Well, I was doing a little basic research to make sure I wasn't conflicted out from helping you and I came up with some weird discrepancies in the public records and social media."

"So you called in an industrial-strength PI on my behalf?"

"Honestly, it took me a little while to get there. At first, I wondered if maybe you were scamming Tayanita. You know, like some elaborate cat-fishing job or something."

"Why would you think I wasn't who I said I was?"

"The puzzle pieces weren't fitting together the way I expected. I know Tristan here has quite a bit of experience, both personal and professional, with that kind of stuff. So I called them in. He's covered under my liability insurance because I contract with Identity Bank quite frequently."

I turn my head towards Tristan as I ask, "Personal experience?"

"Yeah, remember I told you Rogue and I met during a case? Her twin sister, Ivy, was actually my client. Ivy thought Rogue was cat-fishing her over the computer."

"Okay, that explains Tristan's role in this, well enough, I suppose."

I swing back around to face Mark. "So, why are you helping? Do you still carry some sort of torch for Tayanita?"

"I took the case because Tayanita was confident enough to ask for my help. It took her a long time to get there, but she was more interested in helping you than she was afraid of the awkwardness between the two of us. I took that as a sign she finally has the perspective to move on. I hated seeing her stuck in the past and blaming herself."

"If you don't mind me saying so, hearing the two of you talk about each other makes a person wonder if you might still be in love."

"I do love Tayanita. I suppose I always will," Mark admits. When he sees me bristle at his words, Mark adds, "Wait, there's more. The reason I will always love Tayanita is because she was my first real friend. Everyone else in my life always wanted something from me, but not Nita. So, we thought we could make it as a couple. Unfortunately, those kinds of bonds are not strong enough."

"But you're both older now; you could probably make it work," I suggest.

I wish I could see his reaction. Still, I hear him take a deep breath before he answers, "I know it looks like that.

If I were in your shoes, I would feel the same way, but there isn't any spark between Tayanita and me. Truth be told, there wasn't much of a spark even back in the beginning. We were too different."

"So, why take the case?" I press.

"I took the case because Nita asked for my help. She has made many personal sacrifices to help Shelby and me have a good relationship. I want to pay it forward. The bottom line is it's time for me to repay the favor."

"So this whole debacle with the employment agency wasn't some maniacal plot to drive a wedge between Tayanita and me?"

"No! I want Nita to be happy more than anything. You seem to be a perfect counterbalance for her. If I can remove barriers in your life to make it easier for you guys to be together, then that's what I need to do. All those years ago, she helped me get through law school, and I can't thank her enough."

"Okay… But —"

"I think what he's saying is he isn't being nice to get your girlfriend back. He understands he's had his chance at her and they both moved on."

"Exactly, I meant to say what Tristan said. I'm not that succinct," Mark says with a wry laugh.

"Okay, I'm going to choose to believe you, because I believe in Tayanita. Even so, if I see evidence to the contrary, you and I will have to talk again."

"I hear you, but Nita and I are good as co-parents, nothing more," Mark insists.

"Are you guys done hashing out that issue?"

"I've got my questions answered. Mark, I'm glad we

had this talk. I think Ketki will be thrilled. She worries about us not getting along."

"She hasn't said anything to me. How do you get her to share her secrets? With me, she's all teenage girl and attitude."

"I have no special skills. I bribe her with pizza," I quip.

"Sounds reasonable."

"Is there anything else we need to talk about?" Tristan asks as he takes a bite of pizza.

"Actually, there is. I want to know about the job and why you offered it to me."

"What about it?"

"Do you need an employee or are you making a pity hire because I am in love with Tayanita? She told me all of you watch out for each other and take care of each other. I am wondering if that's what's happening here and no one is saying anything."

Tristan clears his throat lightly. "It is true; we do help each other often, that's not what's happening here. I am being stretched far too thin, and I need some people whom I can trust to come in and help me with management. My company has grown exponentially over the past few years, and my staffing has not. We are putting in frightening amounts of overtime and my wife is complaining. Rogue would like to see me every once in a while. That is why I'm hiring someone."

"Your company is well known and on the rise. Everything I've read indicates Identity Bank is a runaway hit. You shouldn't have any trouble recruiting employees, so why are you even considering a washed-up helicopter pilot?" I ask skeptically.

"First of all, I don't consider you washed up. You've simply been redirected. While I was trying to separate your fake military file from your actual one, I had a chance to study your qualifications closely. You have an exemplary employment record. Your letters of recommendation are impressive, and you've shown an ability to be flexible throughout your whole career. Why would I not want an employee like that?"

"I can name one big factor. I'm still adapting to my new reality. You probably deal with a lot of paperwork in your office. Reading is not my strong point."

"Not surprisingly, given what else I do, our office is paper free. All the files are on the computer," Tristan explains.

"What would I be doing? I want to be contributing and not just filling a slot."

"If you're afraid I've made up a position for you, please don't be. When Ketki and I were recoding the game to make it accessible for you, I realized there is a huge untapped market in the gaming world. I would like to make all my games more accessible. I will bring on some programmers and graphic designers. I need someone to supervise this new division of my company."

"Seriously? Ketki adapted one game for me, and you're planning to build a whole department based on that experience?"

"Yeah, I am. I've made a name for myself by being ahead of the curve. It seems to me as all the kids who were raised on Atari and Nintendo get older, they're going to have more needs for accessible products."

"I'm not sure the community of gamers who are visually impaired are big enough to support a whole division of your company," I reason.

"If you define disability as only visual impairments, you might have a point. There are so many disabilities which could be accommodated. Those with hearing impairments, people with motor impairments that need less controller movement and people with autism like Ketki. She has friends who find it difficult to play games because of being visually and auditorialy overwhelmed. I can see developing a special version of the software to combat those problems."

"Big vision for a small company; I'm impressed. What if it doesn't pay off?"

"I've made enough money off other products that it doesn't matter if this is a huge moneymaker, or makes any money at all. Sometimes you do the right thing simply because it's the right thing to do."

"I have one last question. If I start work for Identity Bank, can you still go after the people who tried to sabotage my career?"

"I don't see any reason we couldn't. In fact, we're already working on it," Tristan assures me.

"Okay, consider me your newest employee. There's a perk in it for you. You don't have to give me an office with a window."

"At Identity Bank, everybody gets windows. I don't play favorites."

"You sound like my kind of supervisor. I can't wait to get started."

Tristan reaches out and touches my hand before he shakes it. "Welcome aboard. I think you're going to be an asset to my team."

"One more thing," I add. "I apologize for my skepticism. I was having a hard time figuring it all out from where I sit."

"It's not a problem. I would feel the same way if I were in your shoes," Mark responds as he also shakes my hand.

"Are we good?" he asks.

"I think we are good," I answer. To my surprise, I realize for the first time in a long while, I truly am.

# CHAPTER TWENTY-THREE

# TAYANITA

"Hey, Nita!" Leslie calls across the break room, "Did you see what's on your desk?"

I shake my head. "No, I haven't been in there yet. I came in here to hit up the vending machines. I'm starving."

"Oh good! I didn't miss it!" she exclaims with a squeal.

"Miss what?" I ask, confused by her reaction to the fact I have the munchies.

"Food can wait! Come on; I need to show you something."

Leslie drags me by the arm through the break room and toward my office. When we reach my office, she flings open the door. "See! Isn't that the best?"

Looking around my office, I notice there is a huge potted plant in the middle of my desk complete with heart-shaped balloons.

"Oh my Gosh! They're forget-me-nots. How sweet is that?" Leslie exclaims as she fans herself dramatically. "Who are they from? I need a guy like that in my life."

"Just a random guess, but I'm sure they're from my boyfriend, John. Blue is one of his favorite colors."

"I thought you said he was blind. How can he have favorite colors?"

I frown slightly. "Les, John wasn't always blind. He had an accident; he still remembers what colors look like."

"It's too bad he can't see how gorgeous you are. He's missing out."

I chuckle softly. "You never know. John's fantasy version of me could be far better than the real thing."

Leslie shrugs. "You're so pretty. I don't know how that could be true."

"John has an active imagination. Anything is possible."

"Go on! Read the card. I want to know what it says. We hardly ever get flowers around here."

I open the small gift card and I smile. "I can't believe he remembered. He had these delivered one year to the minute after we met on the phone."

"So, these are for your anniversary?"

"Well, I suppose it's an anniversary of sorts. We have nothing official between us," I explain.

"Girl! Why the heck not? Guys like him are hard to find. You should see what's in the dating pool."

"Oh, I know. Before I met John, I didn't venture into the deep end of the pool very often."

"What are you waiting for? Grab that man and don't let go!"

Leslie's beeper goes off and she looks at me with

frustration. "Darn it! I need to go. I wanted to be here when you called him to say thank you."

"With all due respect Leslie, I think that's something I would rather do in private. This is not the office football pool."

Leslie blushes. "Sorry! I'm a sucker for romance and I have very little of it in my own life right now. So, I'm living vicariously through you."

"Okay, I'll be sure to keep you up-to-date on any wildly romantic developments. You better go. That sounded like a page from Dr. Harris's office. He's probably running late again to deliver a baby."

"You be sure to tell me if you get engaged or anything today. I totally live for that kind of stuff," she instructs as she turns to go out the door.

"Les, this is a potted plant. What about that spells engagement?" I yell after her.

"Guys are funny. You never know. Just be prepared," she teases as she walks quickly away.

I sink down into my office chair and read the card again.

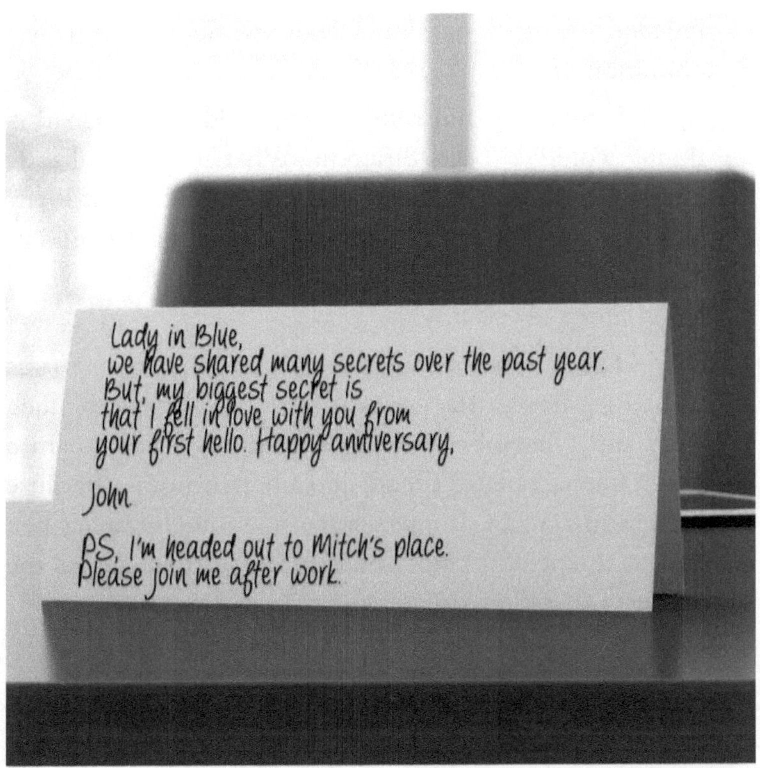



I stare at the card for a while. If I were to think back and try to decide when I actually started falling in love with John, I don't know that I could pick a specific point. It could have been when he gave me permission to be myself and didn't judge what he'd heard or when he had such a great sense of humor about the job he clearly hated. Maybe it was when his sister was injured and he turned to me for comfort. I don't know. All those moments seem monumental and inconsequential at the same time.

I never intended to fall in love with John. I was afraid to open myself up to the pain again. Yet, conversation by conversation, I found myself unable to imagine life without him. I suppose that is the truest definition of love.

I can't help but think what would've happened if things would've been different. What if I had already been in the tub and ignored the phone call? What if my exposure to HIV had been more severe and I would've caught the virus? What if he had hated everything I stand for in life?

The number of things that had to go right for us to be together is astronomical. I can't believe how much John and I have both changed in the last year. I am a better nurse, a better friend, and a better mother because John is in my life. It amazes me how much impact he's had on the person I am. I pick up the plant and smell the flowers as I reflect on how lucky I truly am.

By the time I pull into the driveway at Hope's Haven, I'm more than a little harried. The afternoon surgeries started late. We ran behind all day and never quite dug ourselves out of the hole. There was road construction on the freeway and the heater in my car is acting up.

Jessica greets me. "Somebody is getting anxious. He's been waiting for you to get here. It almost seems like he's nervous or something. I tried to explain to him that Tuffy is a great dog and everything is going to be fine."

"Tuffy?" I ask as I get out of the car and try to stretch my back. "Who or what is Tuffy?"

"Tuffy is a guide dog who went through our program when it was in Kansas. His owner retired to Florida and recently passed away from cancer. His family wanted to know if we could take Tuffy back and give him a chance to be a working dog again."

"I thought you guys just recently started training service dogs," I ask.

"Usually, we train search and rescue dogs, but when Tuffy was a puppy, he followed Devon and Mitch around like a little parasite. So, Mitch worked with the folks from the National Federation for the Blind and got in touch with some other dog trainers who specialize in guide dogs. Tuffy was from our second graduating class of dogs."

"Is Tuffy going to be okay? I read somewhere when a dog has a bond that close with someone, they can become depressed like human beings."

"That's true, but we've been monitoring him for a couple months. He seems ready to work again."

"What does John think of him?"

"Well, you know how guys are. They usually try to play it cool and pretend falling in love with a dog isn't a big deal."

The way she says that cracks me up. I laugh out loud. "Are you telling me my boyfriend has only been here a few hours and he's already in love with the dog? I can't believe I've been replaced so soon."

Jessica gets a somber expression on her face as she says, "Tayanita, I know you were joking but if this works out, John and Tuffy will be inseparable partners. Are you okay with that?"

"Absolutely! John has been looking forward to being more independent. After you made the offer of a guide dog, John has been doing extensive research into how to best utilize a dog. He is so excited about the possibility of going hiking like he used to."

"Doesn't he go hiking and run with you and Ketki? I thought Ketki was telling me about that a few months ago," Jessica states.

"He does. But, he's self-conscious about being attached to us with the rope."

"I can imagine why he would be. Tuffy will help him have more independence," Jessica explains.

"I guess there's only one thing to do. I need to go meet the dog that stole my boyfriend's heart."

As I enter Jessica's open kitchen, I can see John relaxing on the couch with Tuffy at his feet.

"Oh my Gosh! You're a genetic mess aren't you, boy?" I exclaim as I examine the dog.

"Who me?" John jokes.

I regard my very handsome boyfriend with his rugged jaw and shiny short cropped hair. "No, I definitely wasn't referring to you. I think you are genetic perfection. However, your dog here is a bit of a mixed-up mess."

John shrugs. "He feels like a normal dog to me."

"Tuffy is cute. There is no escaping that, but he is a bit unusual. He is the color of a Presto log with a dark snout. He looks kind of like a German Shepherd, but he has Lab ears. One of them sticks up and the other lays down flat."

"There's a funny story about Tuffy. He is a Lab and German Shepherd mix. We used to take him to my father-in-law's church. One of the kids couldn't say Scruffy so, he became Tuffy instead."

"What do you think?" John asks me earnestly, with a hopeful look on his face. "Do you think he would fit into our little family?"

"I don't know. I'm not sure how he gets along with cats and Corkscrew might be a little territorial," I remark.

"Tuffy is thoroughly cat tested. We can't have our service dogs running after small critters. It's bad for business."

John makes a clicking sound with his tongue. Tuffy stands up and waits as still as a statue.

"Blue, watch this. This is so great!" John exclaims as he grabs a hold of the leather handle on the harness. "Tuffy, backdoor — forward."

With deliberate care, Tuffy begins to wind through the furniture and head toward the back door. I am surprised how confident John looks next to the dog. Usually he is not this way anywhere except home.

"Can you catch the door for me?"

I open the door and look out onto the back porch. "John, do you want me to grab your cane? There are steps here."

"No, that's what I wanted to show you. You know how much I absolutely hate stairs? Tuffy and I have already figured it out."

I stand back and watch silently as John uses the dog to maneuver up and down the stairs three times.

"Isn't that amazing?" John asks. "I haven't felt that comfortable in a strange environment since before I lost my vision."

I have to swallow my tears. "That's great, John. I'm

impressed you guys are such strong partners already."

"We were a little surprised about how quickly it happened with your team. I was a little afraid Tuffy would be reluctant to bond to John, but it seems like a natural pairing."

"It's unusual for them to be so in sync, isn't it?"

"In some ways, yes. But, Tuffy is an experienced guide dog. He was looking for an excuse to get back to work. John is a good candidate for a dog because he has a good sense of spatial relationships."

"I don't know if that's my hiking background or if it's my experience as a pilot that's responsible, but in any case, I'm glad I'm not a total klutz."

"Obviously, he's perfect for you. You know me, I don't believe in coincidences. You need him as much as he needs you. It's a match made in heaven."

"I agree," he answers before turning to Mitch. "So, what do I need to do to be able to take Tuffy home?"

"I know you and Tayanita are good friends of ours. Unfortunately, the company that insures Hope's Haven doesn't take my word for it that you're a good person. I need you to fill out some forms for me to make this legal and above board."

"I totally understand. Can we do it now?" John asks eagerly.

Mitch looks over at Jessica. "Do we have enough time to do it before dinner?"

Jessica nods. "I still have to cook the cornbread, so you should have enough time."

"Okay, John — let's go make you a dog owner."

John is incredibly fidgety at dinner. I've never seen him so excited. He's like a kid waiting for Christmas morning. Mitch is reviewing commands Tuffy already knows and is talking with John about some custom training for our hiking and jogging trips.

Without warning, John announces to Jessica, "I hope you have plenty of dessert, I invited a bunch of people over."

"Invited people here?" Jessica asks in a confused voice.

John shrugs. "I thought it would be a good idea for Mitch to explain to the people in my life about interacting with guide dogs. I hope you don't mind."

"Of course I don't mind. I've got plenty of food."

As if on cue, the doorbell rings.

"I guess I'll go get that," Jessica mumbles.

I look over at Mitch to see if I can figure out what's happening, but he shrugs.

Ketki bursts into the room followed closely by Shelby and Mark.

"I want to see the dog," she asserts. "Does he look anything like Hope and Lexicon? Those are two cool dogs."

The doorbell rings again and Mitch gets up to open the door.

"More guests for you, John?"

Katie steps forward and introduces herself, "Hi my name is Katie and these are my parents."

After all the proper introductions are made, John stands up and taps his knife against his glass.

All the sound in the room stops as we all look at John.

"I apologize in advance, but I brought you all here under false pretenses. Although, the idea of a class on working with service dogs would be a good idea."

"False pretenses? Does that mean you're not getting a dog?" Ketki asks as she starts to get visibly upset.

"No, kiddo. That's not what I meant it all."

"What did you mean, then?" Ketki replies.

John winks at her. "It means I fibbed a little to get you all here in one spot."

"Jonathan! I taught you better than that," protests his mother.

"It's for a good cause, I promise," John says. He puts his hand in his pocket and comes out with a box.

*Oh my Gosh, was Leslie right?* I think to myself as John gets up and comes over to my side.

Before I can completely process what's going on, John is kneeling in front of me.

"Tayanita Moya, will you please do me the honor of being my wife? This past year has been one of the best I've ever had. I cannot imagine building a future without you. We found each other when I was a shell of a man drifting through my life with as little conflict as humanly possible. Having you in my life has given me the courage to reach for my dreams when other people say it's impossible and has allowed me to accept my limitations, even the ones I place on myself because I feel guilty."

I'm trying hard not to cry over his sweet words. I never thought I would be in this position. He is everything I wanted in a partner and didn't know I needed.

"Tayanita Moya, I love you and I would love to be your husband," John says as he holds up the ring in my direction.

Ketki shrieks. "*Etsi*, you have to say yes. John is the best thing to ever happen to us as a family."

"I'm aware. That's why I love him. He is perfect for me," I patiently explain.

"Are you going to answer him?"

"Please tell my son 'yes'. We would love to have you as a daughter-in-law. We think you're brilliant," John's dad adds.

I throw my head back and laugh at the absurdity of the situation. I still can't get over the fact Leslie was right.

His mom looks a little taken aback by my laughter as she says, "Our son is still a big catch. Don't let anybody tell you otherwise."

"I know that too, Mrs. Ashford," I respond. "Your son is a spectacular man."

"If I'm so spectacular, why haven't you answered me?"

"Yes, Jonathan Ashford, I will marry you. Like we talked about many times before, having you in my life strengthens me. Together, we should be able to accomplish anything," I answer.

"This means you guys are going to get married,

right?” Ketki responds.

“It’s a little early to know all the details, I asked your mom less than three minutes ago, but that’s the plan, yes.”

Ketki turns to Shelby and Mark. “You better hurry up and get married. You got people in line behind you. Besides, if you were waiting for *Etsi* to be happy, she looks happy to me.”

I help John to his feet and gather him into an embrace as I kiss him.

“Ketki’s right. I am incredibly happy I will be your wife,” I announce as I examine the sparkly gold band.

# EPILOGUE

# JOHN

FROM THE WAY TUFFY is weaving me through obstacles, it seems like they have changed everything around in this room. I reach out and touch a tablecloth. I suppose this spot is as good as any, so I ease myself down into one of the chairs. There must be a bouquet of roses and lilacs on the table because I can smell them a mile away.

Tuffy's tail starts beating on the floor. "You silly puppy! I'm not supposed to pet you because you're wearing your harness today," Ketki remarks as she slides into the chair beside me.

"Hey, Ki, what's up?"

"*Etsi's* hair is up. You should see it. She has a bunch of curls piled on the top of her head. It took the lady forever to do it, but she looks beautiful. I was going to have the same hairstyle, but after I saw how long they took to do Tayanita's hair, I decided to curl mine with a curling iron."

"What is everybody wearing?"

"OMG! Don't get me started on the dresses. It took us forever to find them. *Etsi* decided she wanted hers to be long and blue. Don't tell anybody, but she's picky."

I don't know why, but Ketki's words make me feel totally emotional. I am touched Tayanita tried to match the vision of her I described so long ago.

"I decided I liked blue too, so my dress is kinda like hers, except not quite so grown-up. Tayanita's dress doesn't have a back. Shelby thought my dad would have a cow if I wore something like that. So my dress is the same color but a different style."

"What color are Rogue and Jade's?" I ask, making random conversation.

"That's the funny thing, Shelby had planned for a whole different kind of wedding. But after *Etsi* chose her dress, Shelby decided she loved it so much she asked the others if they would mind wearing blue dresses like Mom's."

"I bet you all look stunning," I remark.

"It's weird. I'm usually a tomboy. I don't like to wear dresses, but this is kind of fun. You should see the shoes I'm wearing. They have a heel — a big one."

"Maybe I should loan you Tuffy so you don't trip and fall," I joke.

"That would be so cool. It would be like the second wedding I've been in where there are dogs."

"Who else had dogs in their wedding?"

"Jessica and Mitch had Hope and Lexicon in their ceremony. After all, it was Hope who brought them together. It was really cool. I got to walk up the aisle with him. I hated the shirt I wore at that wedding because it itched. I don't remember much else. I was still young."

"Don't you remember, Ki?" Mark asks as he walks up on the other side of me. "I asked Shelby to marry me that day."

"Yeah, and then you guys took forever to get married," Ketki remarks.

"That's true enough. Life had a way of getting in the way for a while," Mark replies.

"Well, I hope it happens today. I'm tired of waiting."

"You and me both, Ketki, you and me both." I can hear the smile in his voice. "By the way, I'm supposed to tell you your two moms need you for pictures with the bridal party."

"Okay, bye-bye John," Ketki responds as she runs away.

"Boy, do I know how to clear a room, or what?" Mark quips as he slumps down in a chair next to me. "Hey, I'm sorry you're not part of all this, but I promised one of my legal partners years and years ago if I ever got married, he could stand up for me."

"I understand. You haven't known me that long. You should be able to have whoever you want in your wedding."

"Hey, how is your new job going?"

"It's great. Tristan and Ketki are in the process of creating a different game which features characters with different disabilities. Even better, it looks like we might get a grant for the project," I respond.

"I gotta hand it to you; you have stepped up for Tristan. He says his business has never run smoother."

"Well, I'm not sure I deserve all the praise. Sometimes I feel like I am a round peg trying to fit into a square hole. I was a casual gamer before I was injured, I didn't have the type of experience Ketki has. There's been a huge learning curve. Tristan teases me that once I get the gaming part down, he's going to cross-train me in surveillance work because I'm good at hearing subtle changes in people's voices."

"I bet you would be great on that end of things too. By the way, I know I'm not supposed to see the bridal party today, but I snuck a glance when I dropped off Ketki's new shoes. I have to tell you, I have never seen Tayanita look so happy. Even when she was with me, she wasn't like this. You have brought out a whole other, softer side of her. There will be a big debate today about whether your fiancé or my wife is the most beautiful. Blue is really her color."

"That's what Ketki was telling me. I know I have a picture of Tayanita in my mind, but I bet she's even prettier in person."

"It's true, Nita has always been beautiful. Now that she has gotten help to rectify her past, she is positively glowing."

A chime goes off on Mark's phone. "Oh, I've got to go. The cake is here. The next time you see me, I'll be a married man," Mark says with a happy lilt in his voice. "I can't tell you how great that sounds. It seems like I have loved Shelby forever."

"I know the feeling, man. When it's right, it's right. Go marry your woman, will you? You are not the only person waiting to get married."

The hustle and bustle of the wedding party comes in waves. Sometimes, the room is buzzing with activity, and other times it's completely silent.

I smell the compelling scent of Tayanita's perfume before she even reaches me. She is all kinds of sexy and soft today.

"I need to go line up with the wedding party, but I want to tell you how much I love you. It's because you're in my life that I'm able to watch my ex-husband get married and know I am getting the better part of the deal."

"I don't know about that. I discovered you're right about Mark. He is a great, decent guy."

"He's a great, decent guy who is marrying someone else who he loves more than the air he breathes. I never thought I would be in the same shoes, but I can't wait to marry you. Who knew one little phone call would lead to bliss?"

"I sure didn't. As crappy as that job was, it brought me the Lady in Blue, and you are about as perfect as they come," I remark.

"In the old days, I would've argued with you and said I don't deserve your love, but now I'll just say, 'Thanks. I love you too'."

When Tayanita told me Jessica's grandfather was flying in to officiate the wedding, I was surprised. Florida is a long way away from Kansas. However, after witnessing the ceremony, I can understand why they made the effort to get him here. My sides hurt from laughing so hard. He even offered to get Tayanita and me involved in the act. Walter insisted two-for-one weddings are cheaper and Blue and I should get hitched to save money.

Honestly, I thought about it for a brief second. But

I know her parents would be terribly upset, and my mom would never forgive me if I got married without her being here. Still, it was tempting.

Tayanita walks up behind me and rubs my shoulders as she asks, "What's so funny? I can see your grin from across the room."

"I was just thinking; we should use Walter when we get married. This is the most fun I've ever had at a wedding."

"At least this time, he remembered the rings. He forgot them when Jessica got married."

"Wow! That must've been awkward."

"Not as much as you would think, because Walter is who he is."

"He is a consummate storyteller, for sure. It's almost hard to remember Mark met Shelby in one of the darkest periods of her life. Walter made it all sound like it should be a Disney movie."

"I wonder what he'll make of our story. I still can't believe my luck. Thank goodness for tacky vinyl siding and cold calling. I can honestly say, they changed my life for the better," I comment as I kiss the inside of her wrist.

Tayanita draws in a quick breath. "Amen, you can say that again. When we get a new place, do you think we should put vinyl siding on it in tribute?"

"Nah, I wouldn't be able to see it anyway. I like to value what's on the inside. Finding the person behind the Lady in Blue was like the ultimate treasure hunt. I think your soul is as beautiful as you are on the outside. It doesn't matter how much you dress up, I can see the true you, and I am totally in love with the person you are."

"I never thought I would say this, but I like me too."

"Come on … you're supposed to be totally in love with yourself," I tease.

"Let me rephrase: I am totally in love with the person you see me as because you make me feel perfect," Tayanita says as she leans over and kisses me.

"That was always the goal," I admit before I deepen the kiss.

Ketki runs by. "Eww! You guys are always kissing like Mom and Dad. I guess I'll have to make sure you guys get married too."

"That's the plan, Ki," Tayanita responds as she tries to catch her breath.

"Oh cool! Then I'll have two moms and two dads. Works for me," she announces as she dashes off.

"Works for me too," I whisper in Tayanita's ear. "Let me know when and where."

"Okay, it's a deal. Now that I have my past in perspective, the future looks amazing," Tayanita replies before she gives me a hot, passionate kiss.

Even though I can't actually see my future, I think it looks magnificent.


THE END (for now)

The story of John's sister, Katie, continues in Pieces available now.

# Note from the Author

Dear Reader,

Thanks for reading *Rectify*. If you liked reading characters facing unique challenges…

… there's more.

This just isn't Katelyn Ashford's year.

First, she was shot.

Then the man she thought she loved terrorized her on her own wedding day.

She became a runaway bride.

When she wakes up in a stranger's bed, she can't decide if she's still fleeing trouble or running straight toward it.

As head of security for one of the biggest pop stars in the Pacific Northwest, Logan Anthony knows trouble when he sees it.

So, why can't he resist this prickly bundle of sass wearing a tattered wedding dress?

Why does he always have to be the one to pick up the pieces?

*Pieces* is a sweet romance which will have you sitting on the edge of your seat and rooting for love every second.

Rectify

Get Pieces now in paperback, e-book version or read for free through Kindle Unlimited.


~Mary


Because love matters, differences don't.

# ACKNOWLEDGEMENTS

TAYANITA HAS NEVER BEEN a character who is easy to love. She has layers of pain combined with absolute brilliance. That combination makes her story difficult to tell. However, I think it's important to share the rough times too.

I know this might sound silly because these are not real people, but they feel that way when I write them. I was lucky, I did not struggle with postpartum depression or psychosis. However, I have friends who fight it every day. I wish to thank everyone who was brave enough to share so many deep, personal stories. It's not always easy to admit when you feel weak and helpless. Yet, without your stories, my fictional tale would not be nearly as complete.

I wrote this book for every mother who struggles. We spend so much of our time pretending to be perfect or that our pain does not matter, we sometimes get lost. I want to help remove the stigma from depression, mental illness and disability. Motherhood is hard enough without us judging each other for what we think we would've done in someone else's shoes. The bottom line is, you can't know what it's like unless you been there. If you have been there, I need you to know postpartum depression is not something to be ashamed of. I'm proud of your ability to overcome obstacles no one else can see.

During the writing of this book, my friend Carol Barker passed away from complications of quadriplegia. She was a phenomenal attorney, mentor, and disability advocate. Knowing her made me a better person and I hope to carry on her commitment to diversity and inclusion.

As always, I would like to thank my team of beta readers and critique partners. Your work makes my work shine.

Without the support of my family, Leonard, Brandon and Justin, this book would not have come together. Thank you so much.

~Mary

# RESOURCES

*This resource guide is not intended to be all-inclusive, but rather a collection of websites I think are helpful.*

**Postpartum Progress**:

http://postpartumprogress.org/

This is the charity I chose to receive 15% of the net profits from the sale of this book. It seeks to help remove the stigma of postpartum depression and serve as a resource clearinghouse and source of information about this a debilitating condition. It has excellent resources and advice.

**National Federation of the Blind**:

https://nfb.org/

This website is a comprehensive gathering of information for individuals with visual impairments and their families. It offers everything from job listings to pending legislation. Additionally, it gives helpful information about current technology to make coping with blindness easier.

**Assistance Dogs international:**

http://www.assistancedogsinternational.org/

This charity sets out to demystify service dog programs and help set standards for training programs for all service dogs. It serves as a clearinghouse for those seeking service dogs of all types including guide dogs for the blind.

## DAV Charitable Service Trust:

http://cst.dav.org/

The DAV Charitable Service Trust supports physical and psychological rehabilitation programs that provide direct service to ill, injured, or wounded veterans.

The Trust accepts gifts through workplace giving campaigns, including the Combined Federal Campaign and United Way, employee matching gift programs, and similar special giving arrangements, and provides a variety of direct services for America's sick and injured veterans.

In an effort to make a positive difference in the lives of ill, injured, and wounded veterans and their families, the Trust supports:

Programs ensuring quality health care for veterans,

- • Assistance to veterans suffering from Post Traumatic Stress Disorder (PTSD), Traumatic Brain Injuries (TBI), substance abuse issues, and more.

- • Programs enhancing research and mobility for veterans with amputations, spinal cord injuries, and more.

- • Initiatives for evaluating and addressing the needs of veterans from each era of conflict

# ABOUT THE AUTHOR

I have been lucky enough to live my own version of a romance novel. I married the guy who kissed me at summer camp. He told me on the night we met that he was going to marry me and be the father of my children.

Eventually, I stopped giggling when he said it, and we've been married for more than thirty years. We have two children. The oldest is a Doctor of Osteopathy. He is across the United States completing his residency, but when he's done, he is going to come back to Oregon and practice Family Medicine. Our youngest son is now tackling high school and where he is an honor student. He is interested in becoming an EMT.

I write full time now. I have published more than thirty books and have several more underway. I volunteer my time to a variety of causes. I have worked as a Civil Rights Attorney and diversity advocate. I spent several years working for various social service agencies before becoming an attorney.

In my spare time, I love to cook, decorate cakes and of course, I obsessively, compulsively read.

I would be honored if you would take a few moments out of your busy day to check out my website, MaryCrawfordAuthor.com. While you're there, you can sign up for my newsletter and get a free book. I will be announcing my upcoming books and giving sneak peeks as well as sponsoring giveaways and giving you information about other interesting events.

If you have questions or comments, please E-mail me at Mary@MaryCrawfordAuthor.com or find me on the following social networks:

Facebook: www.facebook.com/authormarycrawford

Website: MaryCrawfordAuthor.com

Twitter: www.twitter.com/MaryCrawfordAut

www.ingramcontent.com/pod-product-compliance
Lightning Source LLC
Chambersburg PA
CBHW032120180726
48284CB00002B/629